T0363748

Key

Encounters

Key Encounters

AN ANTHOLOGY OF
SOUTH AUSTRALIAN CREATIVE WRITING

Edited by

Lise Mackie

Flinders Writers
in association with

Wakefield Press

Flinders Writers
in association with
Wakefield Press
Box 2266, Kent Town
South Australia 5071

First published 2002

Copyright © the individual authors 2002

All rights reserved. This book is copyright. Apart from any fair
dealing for the purposes of private study, research, criticism or
review, as permitted under the Copyright Act, no part may be
reproduced without written permission.
Enquiries should be addressed to the publisher.

Typesetting and production Michael Deves
Printed and bound by Hyde Park Press, Adelaide

National Library of Australia
Cataloguing-in-Publication entry

Key encounters: an anthology of South Australian creative writing.

ISBN 1 86254 578 2

1. Australian literature - South Australia. 2. Australian literature -
20th century. I. Mackie, Lise. II. Wakefield Press. III. Flinders Writers.

820.8099423

Wakefield Press thanks Arts South Australia and Fox Creek Wines
for their support.

Contents

Acknowledgements

Sponsors

We gratefully acknowledge the generous financial support of

 Flinders University English Department

Flinders University Faculty of Education, Humanities, Law and Theology

 Hyde Park Press

 Imprints Booksellers, Adelaide

 ANZ Bank, Flinders University

 Unibooks

 Coriole Wines

Thanks also to Sally Engelhardt for editing assistance.

Preface

This anthology brings together the work of people who enrolled in 2001 in the Flinders University English Department course *The Craft and Culture of Creative Writing*. You'll find here both prose and poetry, for in this course we encourage students to tackle both. For many this course offers the exciting opportunity for their first attempts to write creatively. This collection offers a broad and fertile diversity of styles, subjects, approaches and techniques representing what (mostly) young South Australians think about themselves and their various worlds.

Lise Mackie has done most of the hard work in transforming a series of individual manuscripts into a fine book. Over the years there have been a number of attractive and very readable anthologies produced by students of the course. This one from the 'class of 2001' sits very well in their company.

We are sure you will find that this collection will not only impress you with its range, amuse, instruct and entertain you with its diverse subjects, but also leave you with an enduring appreciation of the creative talents and energies of young Australians. Well done, team.

Rick Hosking & Syd Harrex
Convenors, *The Craft & Culture of Creative Writing*

Alastair Brown

True Love

'I love you.' Benny whispered the words gently into her ear, as he did every morning when he brought Susan her breakfast. He got to the dining hall early, so he wouldn't have to wait in line, and heaped only the finest morsels onto the plastic tray. Benny was the only one who knew exactly what Susan liked for breakfast and he got antsy when they tried to fill the tray for him, he knew they would only get it wrong. For a long time, the nurse had insisted on bringing Susan's breakfast herself, but she was usually so busy that it could be hours after breakfast before she had the time, so she let Benny do it.

As Susan ate, he filled her in on the latest gossip around the ward; new admissions, things that were said in group therapy sessions, pausing every now and then to massage her throat to help the food down. Susan had a little trouble swallowing by herself.

Usually, with breakfast, Benny would bring a picture he had painted in his arts and crafts time. As he looked around the ward he always wished that it had more colour, more life. The white walls were so blank, so cold and unresponsive that he tried to make the most of things by hanging up his pictures for Susan. He knew she liked them. It made his life brighter when he could make her happy with his pictures and with his stories, sometimes he would just sit and talk to her for hours on end.

It was always irritating when he had to leave Susan and go off to another part of the ward, usually when her family came to visit her. They would sit next to her and mumble a few things, looking real uncomfortable, sometimes read a book at her, all without ever looking into her face. The whole time they were there, they never looked at her and they never touched her, like she wasn't really there. Sometimes Susan's mother would cry. All through this, Benny would stand next to the tattered magazine racks, pretending to read an old copy of *Time* and wait for them to leave.

Sometimes Benny would try to show her family that she was there, that she was listening. He would stroll past them, casual as you please, and throw off a 'Hi, Susan' as he went past, to show them that she was still a regular person. But that only made her mother cry more, and the nurse always told him off afterwards.

The nurse only really took to him, though, when he didn't take his pills after dinner. They made him drowsy and he liked to stay up and talk to Susan for longer. It was real easy to hide the pills under his tongue and then slip them into his pocket later. The thing was that, when he didn't take his pills, Benny started to notice things. He noticed things like how other patients were always watching him, watching Susan, hating them both. It wasn't long before he realised that everyone around him, even the staff, were plotting to hurt him, to hurt Susan too. That was when he started to yell at them, sometimes he threw furniture, but he had to protect Susan. Then came the big men in the white shirts, the men with the needle.

The needle felt like an angry insect had bitten him and Benny would scream and throw himself around, trying to shake the pain away. Then the white shirts would grow and grow and become a tiny room. For hours, sometimes days, the walls would spin and churn, making patterns. The voices would come. Benny would start to yell at the voices. He would yell and yell until his voice was hoarse and the voices would yell back. They got louder and louder until the walls began to shake from the noise. Then the yelling would change, the walls would stop moving. And Benny would realise that he was yelling at himself. Then he would sleep.

Sometimes it took a couple of days before Benny woke up after they stuck him with the needle. He'd wake up in the seclusion room, strapped to a bed. After a while, one of the doctors would come and talk to him, like they did during the monthly check up. Benny didn't like the monthly check up, when the doctor walked slowly around the ward with a weaselly little man carrying a clipboard scuttling along behind him. What really used to make Benny angry was how he would shine that little torch into Susan's eyes, then lift her arm and let it drop into her lap like a dead bird. Then he would turn to the scuttling man and say, 'Patient totally unresponsive, continue medication.' And then get up and leave. It used to make Benny really angry, but not any more.

Benny knew now that he was the only one who knew Susan, the only one who could look into her and see the love shining back at him through those blue and unchanging eyes. He knew that, one day, he would walk past and call out, 'Hi, Susan,' and she would call out, 'Hi, Benny,' right back and everyone would stare. That would show the nurse and the doctor and the scuttling man and especially Susan's family that they were meant to be together.

Thinking this, Benny was smiling when he walked back into the ward, he walked straight up to Susan, then sat down and took her cold hand in his own. Susan was staring straight ahead, at a bare patch of wall, so he turned her head slightly so she could see one of his pictures and then leaned in close to her.

'I love you,' he whispered.

Absolutely Nothing

A rich man, middle aged and wearing a well-tailored suit.

A man in a leather jacket, with red hair and empty eyes.

A teenage girl, standing over a sink with a packet full of powder.

A man laughing, a cigarette in one hand and five hundred dollars in his pocket.

A young man, trembling in a corner with a scrubbing brush in his hand.

A young woman, holding a glass of wine and talking about nothing.

A boy at a bus stop, talking to himself.

A young girl walking, trying desperately to be.

What do they have in common?

S tanding in front of his window, all he could see were possibilities. The woman on the news assured him that the world was filled with people. People who strived and fought and lived and died. People who had dreams.

All he could see were possibilities.

'Excuse me sir.' His secretary, Vanessa, on the intercom. 'There's a Mister O'Brien to see you.'

He turned from the window immediately. 'Excellent, excellent. Please send him in.'

His desk was solid oak, hand crafted, and had cost a small fortune to have made. It was his pulpit. It was the mount from which he proclaimed his commandments. From its lofty heights, Donald Cash was, effectively, God. It was there, simply, to impress.

The man who subsequently entered the office sat heavily

and placed both boots squarely on the edge of the desk. He was clearly not impressed.

'You got a job for me?' he asked, in a broad Irish accent.

This, Cash quickly decided, would not do.

There was a large manila folder on the desk, Cash opened it and began to read. 'Thomas O'Brien. Born in Dublin, 1968. Wife; dead. Daughter; dead. From what I understand, after the bombing they had to pick them up with a sponge.'

The man didn't move, but there was fire in his eyes. 'Do you have a point?'

'Oh, I always have a point, O'Brien,' Cash smiled. 'Remember that.' He glanced down at the folder again, and then at the boots on his desk. 'I see you take a size nine.'

The boots were quickly removed.

'Excuse me sir.' Vanessa again. 'Your daughter's on line one.'

'Tell her I'm in a meeting.'

'Very good, sir.'

Cash smiled at the man in front of him. 'Kids, huh?'

No reply.

'Anyway, to answer your question, yes. I have a business proposition for you.'

'Excuse me, Sir.' Vanessa, once again. 'I'm very sorry for the intrusion, but Mister Radley is on line one.'

'Perfect, please put him on.' Cash stood to pour himself a glass of water.

'Lex, hi! I was just about to call you … Really? … Well that shipment should really have reached you by now … No, I'll speed that up personally … Oh and, Lex?' He turned and smiled at O'Brien. 'This time I'll send along … a little something extra.'

*   *   *

Thomas O'Brien ground his teeth as he stood in the elevator on the way down. Normally he took the stairs, but he wanted out as soon as possible. He had worked with some right bastards in his time, it came with the job, but Cash made him want to take a bath.

Ground floor. He was running over the details in his mind as he left the building, Christ but he wished he didn't need the money. But he did.

Then he ran into a girl. He was about to give her a serve for getting under his feet when something stopped him. It was her hair. Light and blonde, curling around her face like strands of sunlight. She looked so much like his daughter that he almost threw his arms around her right then.

Then she spoke.

'Oh, hey. Like … I'm sorry. I was … I was just … yeah. Um, sorry.'

He smiled. 'No harm done. You know, you look … ' He trailed off. 'Yeah, no harm done.'

'I was … um … like, going to the pub for … um … for a drink. Would you … like … um, like a drink?' She pointed to the bar across the road. 'I'm … um … my name is … like … Sondra.'

Thomas considered it for a moment; he could use a stiff drink. But this was one job he wanted over as soon as possible. 'Thanks, but no. I've got to see a man about a dog.'

As he turned to leave, Thomas O'Brien felt like he was losing his daughter, all over again.

As he walked away, Sondra wondered what kind of a dog it was. Probably a big one. He had seemed like that kind of a guy.

She liked the pub, there were always people there. Always lots of people to talk to. And it didn't matter what they said because, in another hour, there would be different people who would say different things. She only ever had one drink, it lasted.

There weren't many people in the pub today because it was only lunchtime, but there was a couple in a booth near the back that looked interesting.

Sondra ordered her usual, she forgot exactly what it was, and then wandered over to say hello. 'Um … hi. I'm Sondra.'

The young woman looked up with a smile, but the young man she was with just shuffled further into the corner. 'Well hi Sondra,' the young woman replied. 'I'm Fleur and this is my brother, Daniel.' Daniel did not look up. 'Why don't you sit down and we can have a chat.'

Sondra sat down.

'So, Sondra. What do you do? I'm in art, I own a gallery near here and I paint a little myself. Nothing spectacular of course but I have my little successes. There was a piece that I painted that was seriously considered for an award once but it simply wasn't to be, you know? So, yes, anyway, what did you say you do?'

'I … um … like … play some music … sometimes. Um … is he … like … okay?' She pointed to Daniel.

Fleur turned to her brother. He was scratching at his forearm. It was red-raw in places and she could see a trickle of blood where he had broken the skin. 'Oh, Daniel! You promised you wouldn't do this! Look at what you've … '

She bit her lip and turned to Sondra. 'I'm very sorry to cut our conversation short, Sondra. But I'm afraid my brother does not know how to conduct himself in polite company.' She turned and dragged Daniel from his seat. 'Let's go then! Are you happy now?'

'Are you? Are you happy that I can't even have a conversation without tying you to your chair?'

Daniel hadn't answered on the way home and he didn't answer now. He just sat and stared at the wall, rubbing his hands as if he were soaping them.

They hadn't warned her about this, they said the medication would calm him down and he would be totally manageable. They hadn't mentioned the nightmares, the delusions, the compulsive cleaning. Just foisted him off on her because they needed the bed! Now he was at the sink, running the water over his hands.

She needed a drink.

In the lounge there was half a bottle of wine and two glasses left over from last night. Fleur filled one, drank, and then filled it again. Staring into the red liquid, she wondered how her life had ended up here. She didn't wonder long, it was too depressing.

On her way up the hall, Fleur glanced into Daniel's room.

He was crouched on the floor, scrubbing at his body with the brush she used on the bathroom tiles. His skin was tearing under the harsh bristles.

'Daniel, stop that!' she yelled, rushing into the room. 'Stop it!' She tore the brush from his grasp and hurled it from the room.

Daniel continued to rub his body frantically, muttering to himself. The only word she caught was 'clean', over and over again.

'Stop it,' she said quietly.

He didn't even look.

'Daniel, stop it.' Nothing. 'Will you just stop it Daniel!' Nothing.

'Stop it, stop it, stop it!' She screamed, hurling the glass of wine at him.

Daniel screamed. He flung himself away, scraping at the wine on his body as if it burned him. He dashed his head against the floor and blood mixed with the wine.

Fleur, tears streaming down her face, ran to him.

'NO! Daniel, no! She threw her arms around him. 'It's okay, no, no, it's alright. Shhh, it's alright.' She rocked and soothed her brother until he slept, and then she began to weep again.

Stumbling to the phone, Fleur punched out a familiar number. 'Hi, Lex? … Yeah, it's Fleur … I need … yeah … can I come round now? … Tomorrow then? … Thanks … Yeah, bye.' Hanging up the phone, Fleur stifled a sob, and sank to the floor.

* * *

'Crazy bitch.' Lex Radley hung up the phone and took a drag from his cigarette.

'So, Heather. You looking for the usual?' The blond teenager in front of him nodded and smiled in a nervous way. She was a looker, but she always paid in cash so he hadn't had a chance to suggest his 'alternative payment' scheme.

Fishing around in a desk drawer, he pulled out a small packet of powder. 'Grade-A Billy Whiz. Just what the doctor ordered.' He handed her the packet in return for a wad of hundred dollar bills. 'Pleasure doing business with you.'

She smiled again. 'Um, Lex. Do you think I could use your bathroom before I go?'

This seemed like a very good idea to Lex Radley, if Heather was stoned he might just be able to slip her one. 'Sure, babe. You know the way.' He watched her retreating form as she walked to the back of the house. Her hips swung as she walked and Lex licked his lips. Very tasty indeed.

He hoped that the new shipment from Cash would come through soon, it was bad for business when he had to turn away customers. The crazy bitch might be a non-stop chatterbox but she was still a customer. Radley was wondering what the 'something extra' Cash had mentioned could be when he heard his front door open. He didn't have any more appointments for today ...

* * *

Heather hurriedly locked the bathroom door and turned to the sink. She hated coming here at all and she wanted to get out as quickly as possible.

She knew he had been watching her, God he was disgusting! The only reason she bought from him was that his stuff was the best. It was cheap too. Lex had once mentioned that it could be even cheaper ... She shuddered at the memory.

Opening the bag carefully, Heather scooped up some of the powder and spread it on her gums. As always, it brought that special thrill. She almost didn't hear the front door closing. Heather froze. No one could find her here. Her father would kill her!

Sidling close to the door, she listened carefully. She heard Lex say something but she couldn't quite hear what. Then she heard another voice.

'Donald Cash sends his regards.' The shock of the words didn't even have time to touch her before two sharp explosions tore through the air.

Heather clapped her hand over her mouth to keep from screaming. It was a long time before she had the courage to open the door. This time she did scream.

Lex Radley lay slumped backwards over his desk, blood pumping from the two holes in his chest.

When she had finished screaming, Heather ran.

* * *

Sondra had been walking back to her flat when the girl ran into her. For a moment she wondered if maybe this time the person would like to go for a drink. But the girl was already running off. It was a pity because Sondra would have liked to know why the girl was running.

Shrugging the question off, Sondra sat down at a bus-stop for a moment.

There was a young boy sitting next to her, clutching a worn backpack. He seemed to be talking to himself.

'Hi. Um … I'm … like … Sondra.'

The boy stopped muttering and looked at her for a moment, then looked down at his backpack. Suddenly, he stood and walked quickly away.

Sondra sat for a while, deep in thought. Why was everyone in such a hurry?

* * *

He walked very quickly, on the edge of a run. He bumped into people, cars honked at him as he jogged across the road, still he walked on.

He was muttering to himself. 'Stupid, so stupid. Why can't you … just stupid … won't let him … so stupid.'

He finally stopped at the front of an office building. 'Cash Enterprises' said the sign on the door. The boy broke into a run as he crossed the foyer, heading straight for the elevators. The doors closed behind a blonde girl that got in just before him. The rest were all busy, the boy ran towards the stairs.

* * *

'Excuse me, sir,' came Vanessa's voice over the intercom. 'Your daughter is here to see you.'

Donald Cash frowned at the briefcase full of money in front of him, then over it at Thomas O'Brien. 'Tell her I'm in a meeting.'

At that moment the office doors burst open to admit a teenage girl. She was crying.

Cash stood, like an angry Zeus behind his desk. 'Heather, I am in a meeting!' he snapped.

'You bastard!' The screamed words hung in the air, neither father nor daughter believing they had been spoken.

'I beg your pardon?' The words were spoken quietly but carried a deadly promise.

Heather floundered. 'You, you killed him. Why? Why did you … was it because of me? Because he sold me drugs?'

Suddenly, Cash laughed. 'You're talking about Radley! Oh, God no, honey. I had no idea you were a junkie. Radley was just business.'

Tears stung Heather Cash's eyes. 'I'm not … '

'A junkie?' countered her father. 'Well I beg to differ, honey. Now, I'm in a meeting so take this,' reaching into his pocket, Cash pulled out a sheaf of bills and handed them to his daughter, 'and go buy yourself some uppers or something.'

Heather threw the money back into his face. 'You make me sick,' she snapped.

Her father's hand struck her cheek sharply, causing her to fall back into a chair.

'You should treat your daughter better.'

Cash froze. This last statement had come from O'Brien. He clenched his teeth in rage.

'That's it!' he yelled. 'I will not be preached to by a hired murderer and a drug addict! You!' he jabbed a finger towards O'Brien. 'Take your money and get the fuck out of my office!'

'And you,' he waved his hand disgustedly at Heather, 'just get the fuck out.'

Turning away, Cash stared out of the window until he heard them leave. He stared into the possibilities.

A few moments later, Cash heard his door open again. He spun angrily. 'I thought I told you … '

But he didn't see his daughter when he turned, neither did

he see O'Brien, or even Vanessa. He saw a boy he didn't recognise, clutching a worn backpack. Then he saw the gun.

The boy's eyes were green over the trembling gun-sight. Donald Cash remembered where he had seen them before.

'So stupid,' mumbled the boy with the familiar eyes.

*   *   *

Heather was standing by the elevator when she heard the gun-shots. Not just two this time. Three, four, she lost count. Heather got into the elevator; she pressed the button for the ground floor. The doors closed.

*   *   *

Sondra sat in her group and talked about her week. 'I ... um ... had a really ... like ... good week. Everything's going well and ... um ... I talk to people a lot. I met ... um ... some really nice people but ... like ... they were all in ... like ... a big rush. I guess they had ... like ... important things to do but ... um ... yeah. I don't have the ... um ... the dreams any-more and ... like ... yeah ... everything's ... um ... it's great. Yeah ... everything's great.'

What do they have in common?

Absolutely nothing.

Bleeding Dry Gin

He sits in a battered armchair, which only has two
legs and a strange stain on the seat. He sits and
laughs at the world. The clock in the corner
chimes twelve for the twelfth time today, forcing him
upright, like a mechanical cuckoo. A laugh bubbles up from
inside him like a mountain-spring,
or like sour vomit.
The laugh dies on his lips as his legs buckle under him, both
hamstrings sliced by an invisible knife, which is wielded by
his past. The glass shatters as he hits the ground and cuts
deep into his outstretched palm. The glass bleeds gin into
the carpet, which is brown, or maybe orange.
The chair is propped up by six red bricks, the kind that can
be used to house
a family of four, or to crush
a skull to pulp.
He lies alone, bleeding gin into a carpet of unidentifiable
colour, and he laughs. He laughs at the world. He laughs at
himself.
He laughs at the two-legged chair and the clock and the
carpet, which might be green. He laughs and he laughs and
he laughs.
Or maybe, he screams.

The hair on his head is orange and it blows in the wind,
tousled by a hand which isn't there. Like his father's hand.
The hair on his head is lank and limp and streaked with
blood when the floor leaps forward to strike him, like a giant
fist. Like his father's fist.
He is tall, so tall that he has to stoop to get through
doorways.
He stoops so far that he folds like a deckchair, or like a bad
hand of poker.

He is thin, so thin that, when he turns side-on, sometimes
people can't see him at all. Just a cigarette, a penis, and a
glass of raw spirits, hanging in nothingness.
He never eats, or sleeps.

The drink in his hand is gin, always gin (they ask him if he
wants tonic and he tells them 'only if there's room in the
glass'). The cigarettes could be any brand but he only buys
the ones which bear the warning he likes:
'Smoking can cause you a painful and premature
death, reduced quality of life and endanger
the health and happiness of all those around you.'
Pain has meticulously plucked out his eyes with greedy
fingers and he views the world with perfect clarity from his
empty sockets. He always speaks the truth, why tell lies when
you can live them?

There's a room in his head, he calls it home. In his home
there is a bookshelf filled with ideals and philosophies which
he no longer believes in, and a television which offers him a
fulfilled life for only five easy payments. Wherever he stands
in his home, he is only ever one step away from the fridge,
one step away from the bed.
The fridge is filled with bottles. Liquid oblivion reaching out
to him with icy arms, which are somehow warm. The arms
of a father who isn't angry
and a mother who cares.
The bed is filled with bodies. Some have faces and some do
not.
Male. Female. Friends. Enemies.
They writhe together like a net of flesh. If he tries to sleep
they will drag him down, suffocate him with their lust and
their need. His only defence is to fuck. Fuck everything and
be fucked by everything and still feel nothing.
He is penetrated in a hundred different places but nowhere
deep enough
to even notice.

He looks at the walls of his home, they are covered with
eyes. Some accusing, some caring, some hating and some
loving. He meets the gaze of every eye with his own empty
sockets. He toasts them with a double gin.
He has another drink, another smoke, and another fuck.
And he screams and he screams and he screams.

Dysfunctional

My mother, she is coming back,
She told me so herself.
My father, he just got the sack,
'At least I've got my health.'
My sister says she's getting hitched,
She told my dad by mail.
My brother phoned me up and bitched,
'Cause dad won't post his bail.
My grandpa, in a mental home,
Dad says that he's a loon.
My grandma, she just sits and moans,
Dad says she'll join him soon.
My auntie, in rehab so it's said,
For being 'on the sauce.'
My uncle got shot in the head,
A suicide of course.
Myself? I'm not at all that sour,
Nor under madness' steeple.
And now I'm up this clock tower,
I think I'll shoot some people.

Morning Has Broken

The most terrifying noise I've ever heard
Greets me every single day,
The harsh buzzing sound at 6 am.
Cutting through the cloudy grey
Of all my pleasant dreams and pleasant thoughts
To drag me back into the world.
So unwillingly, I crack my eyes
As the clock croaks from where it's hurled.

It's time to face another day
It really is a crime.
Morning hasn't just broken. No,
It's really fucked this time.

So I roll out of bed and bang my head
On the wall (on the wrong side),
Stumble and trip through the darkened room
Till I can switch on the light.
The light shoots through my retina, cuts
Right into my brain,
Doing, I'm sure, permanent damage
To my head again.

But it's time to face another day
Though I don't feel worth a dime.
Morning hasn't just broken. No,
It's really fucked this time.

The bathroom floor's already sopping wet,
So too are all the towels.
I slip and bang my head again
With a clatter and a howl.
I shower quickly 'cause the water
Keeps running hot and cold,
Then I almost faint from loss of blood
Because my razor is too old.

So it's time to face another day
If I can just make the climb.
Morning hasn't just broken. No,
It's really fucked this time.

Then to a mug of coffee that's
So strong you have to bite,
And I can taste it mixing with
Those corn chips from last night.
In a giant rush I grab my stuff
And piss bolt out the door,
On the train I realise my wallet's
Still at home on the floor.

It's time to face another day
And don't you wish they wouldn't say
That it will all turn out okay
If you just face it anyway.
Despite the feeling of decay,
The head of mud and feet of clay,
All the disaster and dismay
Is just the price you have to pay
Because the morning's really, really fucked this time.

Hugh Sullivan

Coffee and Polaroids

They sat in the staff kitchen of the Parks Community Outreach Centre.

'You remember Elvin the Croatian?' She lit a cigarette, frowning, looking up at Brawley. 'He used to come in here a bit.'

'I think I remember a Croatian,' Brawley said. He sat back in the chair and looked at the woman. She was in her late twenties, short black hair with copper highlights, tied at the back. She appeared considerably stoned.

'You know,' Brawley said, 'in the month you've been here, I think I've seen you just two or three times.'

'Is that a good thing?'

Brawley looked at the dirtied walls of the kitchen. Some teenagers had scrawled obscenities – a few of which were directed at him – above the sink and on the pantry door. The fridge was padlocked.

'It's not anything.' He paused, ran a hand through his thinning hair, 'I mean, it's definitely not a bad thing.'

The woman smiled and tapped her ash in a floral mug.

'You know I'm here on community service,' she said.

'I didn't know that.'

'Nothing much. Just parking fines etcetera.'

'Etcetera.' Brawley nodded slowly and sympathetically. Social worker reflexes. Above him a fluorescent light began flickering. The woman dropped her cigarette into the mug and walked over to the sink.

'Can you tell I've been chewing on pills?' she asked, picking a dirty mug from the sink and rinsing it under the tap. 'I don't really have a whole lot to do around here. Just answering phones and putting out pamphlets.' She looked at the cartoon on the mug and smiled, 'Garfield.'

Outside the rain had stopped and sunlight was beginning to show through the fine grey clouds. Brawley watched as the woman studied the cartoon on her mug. She laughed a little uncertainly, then turned the mug around to see if there was more. There wasn't, and she laughed even harder.

'You want pills?' she asked.

Brawley shook his head. 'I think that might be giving the wrong message.'

'Right. Drugs and alcohol. I read the pamphlets.'

'Maybe you should take some home. Read them some more.'

'Maybe.' She switched the kettle on and spooned some instant coffee into her mug. 'I still think we should get high, though.'

'I still think we shouldn't.'

The woman sniffed and stood by the window, turning her face to the dilute sky. The rain had dried on the pane and she smiled faintly at the muddied streaks. Brawley looked at the woman; at the thin light on the curve of her neck. He looked at her bare feet and noticed a thin string of beads around one of her ankles. He realised he did not know her name.

'I mean, what do you do around here?' the woman asked Brawley. 'You organise line dancing for junkies?'

'We try to help.'

'You care?'

'I get paid to.' He paused. 'I don't get paid a lot, though.'

The woman looked down at the dirty linoleum floor, tapping her foot in the small puddles that had formed around the sink. She removed a menthol tin from her pocket and took a joint from it.

'Scott's in the dark room,' she said, taking a zippo from the table and lighting the joint. 'He's teaching the mongoloids how to develop photos.' She took several deep tokes and held her breath. 'I was told he's a kiddie-fiddler.' She poured the boiling water into her mug, stirred the coffee, and dropped the spoon into the sink.

Brawley put his elbows on the table and rested his chin in his hands, watching as she pulled a chair close to his own and sat down. 'Who told you that?' he asked.

'And Bitch the receptionist is at the post office,' she said, ignoring him. 'So that leaves you and me to smoke this joint and do whatever.'

She pressed the joint to Brawley's lips. Brawley inhaled and almost immediately began coughing.

'Why don't you tell me about the Croatian,' he said.

The woman was staring at the closed door. She unbuttoned her jeans.

'About Elvin?' She took Brawley's hand and pressed it firmly against her hipster panties, hooking his thumb under the elastic. Brawley looked towards the door. He could hear a telephone ringing from another room.

'Elvin died,' the woman said, smiling. She tried to knot her brow solemnly, but her lips were stuck high on her gums. Brawley watched her dig her nails into her palms, trying to shake the stiff, stoned grin. He considered removing his hand, but decided against it.

'A friend of mine is an orderly at the Q.E.H.,' the woman said. She kept one hand on Brawley's, and the other around the mug of coffee. 'Elvin comes in and he's got a knife just sticking out of his enormous gut; just jiggling when he walks.' She took a sip of her coffee and coughed. 'Anyway, turns out he drank some hydrochloric acid because his wife left him. Problem was, the acid made it feel like his stomach was going to burst, so he stuck himself with a knife to try and release the pressure.'

The woman shrugged and exhaled a thick cloud of smoke. 'So I don't know what he died of exactly. Maybe a little bit of both.' She placed the joint between Brawley's lips, then leant over and unzipped his jeans. 'Would you drink acid if your wife left you?' she asked.

'How'd you know I was married?'

'You've got the eyes,' she said, tracing the lines around Brawley's eyes, bringing her hand down his face, his chest, finally slipping it inside his underwear. 'What's she like?'

Brawley shrugged and drew on the joint. 'Like a wife.'

The woman brought her lips to Brawley's ear. 'Can you hear that?' she whispered, her hand warming against his skin.

Brawley inhaled deeply on the joint and listened. He heard a telephone ringing.

'That could be her,' the woman said. Brawley wasn't sure whether she was mocking him or not. He closed his eyes; then opened them on the fluorescent light buzzing and flickering above him.

'I think … ' he began, but stopped. His head felt heavy, disproportionate. Everything felt disproportionate. He found himself leaning forward, moving to kiss the woman.

'Do you know how old I am?' she asked, drawing away, smiling.

Brawley looked at the woman's face, then at the kitchen and the damp cloud of sour steam and smoke that had gathered around the lights.

The woman's smile widened, though the humour had left her eyes. She patted Brawley's cheek. 'You look like a carnival skeleton in this light,' she said, finishing the joint and letting the smoke fall between herself and Brawley.

Brawley stared in confusion at the smoke and at the obscured face behind it.

'What are you doing?' he heard himself say.

'What are you doing?' the woman echoed, starting to laugh. 'Guess my name.'

'I don't … this isn't good.' His voice came out in a dry, cracked whisper. He was surprised to find his free hand clenched tightly. He removed the other from the woman's grip. 'What are you doing?'

The woman sat back suddenly and cleared her throat. 'I'm only fucking with you,' she said, buttoning up her jeans. She pouted her lips. 'I'm high,' she said. 'I'm fucking with you.'

The woman pinched Brawley's stomach as if he were a child. Brawley slapped lightly at the hand, then harder. Finally the woman stopped and turned smiling towards the door. Brawley followed her look and saw Scott standing in the door-way, lighting a cigarette.

Scott walked across the kitchen and picked a mug from the sink. 'Lucas Brawley,' he said, concerning himself with some dirt at the bottom of the mug, 'what the hell have you been up to in here?'

Scott was a photographer who volunteered his time once a fortnight at the centre. He wore his long blonde hair in a ponytail, and always had two cameras – one a Polaroid – slung around his neck.

'I hope you're going to clean up this mess,' he said, looking at the puddles on the floor and the damp remnants of the joint on the table. He spoke as though Brawley were one of his students. 'Don't worry,' he grinned. 'I'm just fucking with you.'

Brawley felt himself smile. He considered lunging at Scott, encircling his neck with thick, discoloured fingers. He took a sip of the woman's coffee.

'Brawley's way too literal,' the woman told Scott.

'Probably,' Scott nodded. He walked up to the woman and patted the small tuft of hair at the back of her head. 'I'm sorry,' he said, 'I don't think you told me your name.'

'Magic,' the woman announced proudly.

'Magic. That's a beautiful name. Don't you go changing that.'

Scott raised the Polaroid camera and took a photo of Magic. He took the Polaroid and gave it to the woman to shake, then turned to Brawley with the camera.

'Say "China",' he said, and took a photo. As he stood shaking the fresh Polaroid, he looked down at Brawley and let his smile slowly widen. 'One for your kids,' he said, almost sympathetically.

Brawley looked at the developing photo, then down at his jeans. They remained unzipped, his underwear exposed.

'You know, your phone's been ringing a lot the last hour,' Scott told Brawley.

'It's his wife,' Magic said. She looked at Brawley.

'You know,' Scott said to Brawley, 'Dex is in your office. He's been waiting there for a while now.' He turned to Magic. 'Dex lives in a caravan park at Outer Harbour. He's a schizophrenic who likes to keep Brawley up to date with all the nut-job paranoia. You don't want a guy like that answering your phone,' he said, turning to Brawley.

'No, ideally not.' Brawley tried to smile. He was having difficulty with the button on his jeans.

'You mind if I sit here?' Scott sat on the edge of the table, facing Magic. He picked up the remainder of the joint. 'Shit, Brawley, aren't you a little old for this?'

'That's how it seems.'

'He's a little old,' Magic said.

'Yeah, I can see that,' Scott said and laughed. He raised the camera and took another photo. Brawley's face tightened at the flash, his eyes beginning to ache in their sockets.

'Man, you don't look so good.' Scott shook the Polaroid and touched Magic's knee with his foot. 'You wanna smoke out?'

Magic nodded.

Scott turned to Brawley. 'I think I'll leave you to it,' Brawley said. He looked at the photo on the table and flinched at his own stricken image. He pushed his chair back and stood up. There was another flash.

'That might be an idea,' Scott said.

Brawly walked past the fridge, where someone had scratched *Lucas Brawley is a cunt* into the door. He stepped out into the dark hallway and paused as the telephone began ringing from his office.

Suburban Death

'Listen, Dex,' said Brawley, 'this is a community outreach centre. We put on origami classes for recovering alcoholics. What you're telling me – we don't deal with that. It's not our problem. I don't think free coffee and biscuits can help you.'

Dex murmured something. He had fixed his stare on a point somewhere between Brawley and himself.

'You see,' continued Brawley, 'if you really think that some kid in your trailer park has been sent to, what, impregnate your mind with alien propaganda?'

Dex nodded, his chin folding into three as he did so. 'To brainwash me and my brother,' he said. 'The lady – the whore – next door, she pretends the kid is hers. But Ernest and me have reason to believe otherwise.'

'The television set.'

'That's right. The T.V.'

Brawley exhaled loudly through his nostrils and pushed his chair back. Dex and his brother Ernest had been visiting the centre intermittently for three years, each visit prompted by a substance-fuelled paranoia. Fears of Special Ops., surveillance and assassination attempts. This alien child with some evil agenda, however, suggested a move beyond shallow paranoia.

'Jesus, Dex, what kind of madness have you and Ernest been cultivating out there?' Brawley asked.

He was hardly surprised to see the face cloud with sudden fury. It appeared strangely discoloured, the eyes pale and unsound.

'I mean, what do you want me to do, Dex?' Brawley asked. He felt himself entering a place that required caution.

Dex leaned forward, running a soiled tissue across his upper lip. 'If something should happen,' he whispered, 'we may need you. I'm not sure in what capacity yet. Perhaps transport.'

Brawley sighed and swivelled in his chair. The window in his office commanded a view of a vacant lot where the local kids played and the occasional addict overdosed. Today four boys were using a football as an excuse to grind each other into the mud.

'I'm going to give you this number Dex, and I think you should call them.' He copied the phone number from his book and slid it across the table. Dex viewed it fastidiously.

'Why is it, chief, that you refuse to take me seriously?'

'That's not it. I'm just beyond caring.' It was true. Seven years in a community outreach centre had earned him a degree of apathy. 'Dex,' he began, but the man's attention had wandered.

Brawley sat back and looked at the cracks in his ceiling. It was the smallest office in the complex – the hottest in summer and the coldest in winter. The walls had been painted a dark blue that was strangely at odds with the rest of the centre, as though an attempt had been made to conceal some unsightly stain. He had placed a large pine bookshelf in the far corner, and filled its deep shelves with a variety of texts – some clinical, some self-help, though most were fiction: worn paperbacks he had picked up from Ox-fam and bookstores on Leigh Street.

Brawley sighed and looked at the one photo he kept of his wife and two children on his desk. He noticed that Dex's gaze had also fallen on the photo.

'Dig it,' spat Dex. 'Tonight when your sleeping, I'm gonna slit your throat and take to your wife's privates with something blunt and rusty.'

Brawley nodded. He felt his jaw growing numb; something was forming in his throat, and a hollow, fearful grin possessed his features. 'Then it's a date,' he said.

'You're a real fuckin' stupid man, chief.'

Brawley, his face aching under the weight of his own humourless smile, braced himself for pain. Dex was standing above him now, fluorescent-cast shadows bleeding down his face, not looking entirely human. Distant laughter made its way from the vacant lot. Distant laughter and the threat of violence. It reminded Brawley of his childhood.

'I think I really might kill you,' said Dex.

'I won't hold it against you. There's something about me that incites people to violence.'

'Not now, though. Later.'

Dex turned, and Brawley watched as the corpulent mass passed out the doorway. He felt the threat to be an empty one, but remained plagued by some vague thrill of fear.

When Dex had left the building, Brawley picked up his

phone and called the police. Although sympathy was something that had eluded him in recent years, he felt something of a moral obligation to the trailer park child and her mother. He kept the call short, and did not tell them about Dex's promise to kill him.

Brawley spent the remainder of the day reading. When four-thirty came, he decided to leave. He took the daily paper from the tearoom and passed through the lobby. Elise was working behind the reception desk and smiled as Brawley passed. She was mildly attractive, and Brawley indulged in the belief that she wished to sleep with him. The thought occasioned him one of the day's few pleasures.

Outside was absurdly cold. Brawley turned his collar up against the wind and walked towards his car. A strange warmth was coursing through his veins, and he felt perversely alive amongst the grey factory ruins and portable houses.

The street was empty; save his own '83 Laser and a weathered Holden ute in which two shadows appeared to be either wrestling or making love. Brawley unlocked his car with some difficulty. It had been broken into three times, and stolen twice. On one occasion he had come out of the centre to find an emaciated Malaysian asleep on the back seat. It was an odd moment and Brawley – as he watched the Malaysian climb with some difficulty from the window he had smashed – felt a slight admiration for the man's whimsy.

Now, in his car, Brawley sat in silence, interrupted only by the sound of flesh being driven into corrugated iron. He turned to see one of the children crumpled at the base of the lot's fence. The other three stood laughing as the rain began to fall. The emptiness of the lot and its children clung to Brawley as he pulled away from the curb.

It was five o'clock when he turned into the saloon's parking lot. The sun had passed beneath the day's cloud, casting a pleasant glow on the bar's unpleasant parking lot. Brawley entered and ordered a beer. Beside him, a couple of women in their forties moved with fleshy undulations to the music, limbs jerking in a desperate search for the off-beat.

Residual beings, Brawley thought. Residual beings from better nights.

The afternoon glow seemed to stop like some unwanted visitor at the bar's threshold. Patrons sat like extensions of the darkness, their faces lit only by the lurid neon strips lining the bar. Otherwise it was darkness. It occurred to Brawley that here, in the saloon bar drinking beer, it was never light.

'Daylight has the tendency to vulgarise things,' the barman told Brawley. 'Our customers don't need things further vulgarised for them.'

Brawley nodded and ordered another beer.

'Settle a bet, Brawley.' The barman brought his face close to the bar, resting his arm in the small pools of liquor that had gathered on its surface. 'Did Lautrec die of the clap?'

'I don't know.' Brawley looked at the man, surprised by how unwell he appeared in the sickly blue glow. 'But it is treatable these days.'

The barman ran a comb through his thinning hair and allowed a brief laugh to pass over his lips. It went unnoticed in the oily darkness – a laughter measured in thick wheezes and venereal discomfort.

Brawley looked down at the bar, his gaze taken by something scrawled in liquid paper on its surface:

Close your eyes, she said, and listen to life.
But all I heard was cryptic whispers
And the furtive steps of a promise absconding.

He wondered if, in one of his more indulgent moments of self-pity, he had not written it himself; a quaint epigraph for those ordering the first of countless drinks.

Brawley finished his third beer and turned to leave. As he did so, the barman proffered a yellowing grin. A small twitch rippled across his lips but he held the smile and told Brawley to have a nice day, seemingly without irony.

Brawley left the bar feeling hated and a little nauseous.

It was dark when Brawley stepped out into the lot. He walked towards his car, but it was not until he was inside, glancing in the rear view mirror, that he noticed the Holden ute. When he pulled onto the road, the ute's lights came on and, showing little discretion, it exited the bar's lot closely behind him. It continued to follow Brawley off the highway and, when a car pulled in behind the Holden – its lights silhouetting the ute's occupants – he could discern the thick-set frame of Dex riding shotgun.

Brawley kept one eye in the mirror as he negotiated the suburban turns. He took a corner at the last conceivable moment and cursed himself for indicating. Glancing back, he could see the ute turning comfortably behind him. This, he thought, is where it ends: beneath the streetlights; safety houses with their terriers barking, a retirement village. A cheap suburban death.

On a long, empty street that Brawley did not recognise, the ute pulled ahead of him and stopped short. Dexterity and diligence was required to avoid the vehicle. Brawley possessed neither and braked, almost relieved, behind the stationary ute. He turned off his car.

Since spotting the ute at the bar, Brawley had felt the day's intangible aspect gradually return. At first, standing alone outside the centre, he had thought it to be the thrill of fear, some cold abstract funk. Now, watching Dex rise unsteadily from the ute, he took it to be a sense of exhilaration. It consumed his body and charged the cream brick houses that lined the street. Exhilaration in the promise of death. It had been there – surreptitiously – since the afternoon.

Dex reached the car and peered through the open window, 'How's your luck, chief?' His face, lurid beneath the streetlights, sported an almost reptilian aspect.

'I haven't lived the most providential of lives, Dex.'

Brawley received the first blow with a whimper and the second blow much the same. Blood flowed copiously from his nose and gathered in a black puddle in his lap. He thought he felt a thick discharge running from his right ear.

'You're already dead.'

Brawley wasn't sure whether he had heard the words or

not. When he opened his eyes, Dex was already back in the ute.

It was a fifteen-minute drive to his home. He put his car in the garage and remained there, making sure he had stemmed the flow of blood. The dog barked at him from the back yard.

Walking into the house, he felt empty and defeated. No lights were on inside, and he trod on a Lego construction as he entered the kitchen. He turned on the light, drank milk from the carton, and put some ice in a handkerchief. Holding it to his nose, he read a brief note left by his teenage daughter, disowning him as a father. He shifted the ice and placed the note back on the table.

After checking on the baby, he went into the bedroom. His wife was lying half-dressed on top of the covers.

'What time is it?' she asked without opening her eyes.

'Early.'

'I'm sorry. I was exhausted.'

He took off his shoes and sat on his edge of the bed, facing the wall. His wife sniffled.

'I told Will and Penny we'd have dinner there tomorrow.' Her voice sounded thick and carefully measured, as though she had been crying.

' Okay,' he said.

'I tried calling your office today, but there was no answer.'

'No.'

'I called a number of times.'

Brawley put his feet up and rested on the bed, still facing the wall. He was staring at his wife's set of Russian dolls on the mantle. Usually they were placed securely inside one another; but today she had set them, biggest to smallest, across the mantle. Now, lying in the darkness, Brawley felt them scrutinising him with their painted features. He could feel the approach of an almost vertiginous fear of loss. He closed his eyes, but the dolls' prosaic grins remained in his mind's eye.

The Drover's Wife

1.   EXT   AUSTRALIAN OUTBACK   DAY 1

A two-roomed house built of round timber, slabs, and
stringy-bark stands surrounded by stunted apple-trees and
the occasional she-oak. At one end of the house is a big bark
kitchen. A woman, IRENE, stands by the kitchen, watching
her four ragged, dried-up-looking children play about the
house. Suddenly one of them, TOMMY, cries out.

TOMMY: Snake! Mother, here's a snake!

Irene dashes from the kitchen, snatches her baby from the
ground, holds it on her hip, and reaches for a stick.

IRENE: Where is it?

TOMMY: Here! Gone into the wood heap! Stop there,
mother! I'll have him. Stand! I'll have the beggar!

                              *   *   *

Tone Jameson loosened his tie and walked to the window
overlooking Pirie Street. His gaze followed a young female
power walker across the street, shifted focus, and caught a
glimpse of his own damp features in the glass. He turned
back to the man at the desk, who was breathing heavily
through his nose and turning the pages of the script ten at a
time until he had neared the end. He looked up at Jameson.
   'I'm sorry, I've forgotten your name,' he said.
   'Don't worry, a lot of people do. Tone Jameson.'
   'Tone?' he smiled. 'Sounds like a pimp.'
   'It's short for Anthony.'
   'Well, I'm going to call you Jameson.'
   There was another man sitting at the desk, thirty-odd

with a thick upper lip that carried a pencil-line moustache. He had introduced himself as Lucien, and appeared to take some pleasure in doing so. 'Jack,' he said now with a slight lisp, 'what's your view, Jack?'

The man called Jack looked up at Lucien, then at the liquor cabinet by the door.

'You see, sir,' began Jameson, 'what this marks is a return to the seventies renaissance. This is the battler. The pioneer. This is us. Sure she's had a hard life, but when she kisses her boy at the end there, you just … '

'Who'd you have in mind when you wrote the part of Irene?' Jack asked.

Jameson took a short breath. He had prepared for this. 'I had three things in mind when I scripted her: Fortitude, Rectitude, and Maternal Spirit.'

'So … ' Jack worked his hands in the air, finally pointing them in the direction of Lucien, 'perhaps Sophie Lee?'

'Well sir, I think it's essential that the woman have an air of rectitude and fortitude … '

'And breasts,' Lucien breathed. He had carried a bottle of sparkling water, Wild Turkey, and three glasses from the liquor cabinet. 'It's important she have breasts, Tone.' He gripped the bottle of water, decided against it, and instead poured three glasses of neat whiskey. He flicked through the script, pausing somewhere in the middle to drain his glass.

'I think,' began Jameson, 'that an emphasis on breasts would perhaps be missing the point somewhat.'

'You don't think Sophie Lee, then?'

'I think Cate Blanchett would perhaps be better suited to the part,' Jameson said. He leaned over and took his glass of whiskey from the desk.

'Sure as shit she would,' exclaimed Jack. 'Her or Mimi McPherson.'

'What if – when she bends to kill the snake – a breast should pop out of her top?' Lucien cupped his hands in the shape of a breast. 'Just a single tit.'

'Again, I think that would be going against the tone of the piece.'

The colour had risen in Jack's face. 'So both breasts would be out of the question then?' he asked.

'I think it would be.'

'You've got to understand,' Lucien told Jameson, 'that, as financiers, we have to consider the viability of the piece. Not just the tone.'

'And breasts are viable,' Jack said.

'We don't want to get another writer in on this, Tone. Run with us here.'

Jameson placed his glass back on the desk without drinking from it. Lucien eyed the act with faint suspicion. He drained the glass, filled his own with a double measure and looked triumphantly at Jameson. He then took the two fingers in a single gulp and raised a fist to his lips as his upper body shuddered. He smiled out the window as his eyes began to water.

'And I think,' Lucien finally said, 'that where you have this flash back to the ...' he looked down at the script, then back at Jameson '..."gallows-faced swagman" ... Well, I thought: Sexual. Very sexual. Perhaps there could be a development there. Perhaps something sexual.' He turned his head slowly towards Jack, who was nodding solemnly as he lit a joint.

'It was,' he agreed, 'very sexual in nature.'

'Think financial viability, Tone.' Lucien turned to the final page of the script. 'And why, at the end, does the breaking daylight have to be "sickly"? I mean, I'm seeing a triumphant orange glow being cast onto this girl's face, right? Only the orange glow ...,' he grinned widely and turned to Jack, who was smirking with complicity.

'Only the orange glow,' began Jack, his breath held between tokes, 'the orange glow ... ' He exhaled deeply and coughed a little at the end. A broad, dry smile was crawling across his face. 'What the fuck comes next, Lucien?'

'The orange glow, man, it's not from the rising sun.' He removed the joint from Jack's grip and took several deep tokes. 'It's from the fucking fire.'

Jameson felt his back growing cold and damp. 'The fire?'

'That's right. The fire's got hold of the kitchen and it's just this enormous … '

'Fucking, *blaze*,' said Jack, almost reverently. 'It's already consumed, like, two or three of the children.'

'And this bitch with the tits – she's gotta put the damn thing out. You know, she gets all hot and sweaty … '

'And dirty.'

'And her breasts are just, like, you know … ' Lucien indicated a pair of breasts with his hands. Jameson leaned over and poured himself a generous measure of whiskey. Lucien grinned as he did so, wiggling his thumbs so as to suggest erect nipples. 'That shit is viable.'

'*The Drover's Wife*,' said Jack, 'the Aussie spirit. With a fucking fantastic pair of tits.' He grinned at Lucien, and they both turned to Jameson.

Jameson drained his drink.

'Of course, it would take a minor redraft,' he said, and moved to refill his glass.

Watching

Corea

'Every day she's there. I sit in my deck chair on the front lawn and watch her. She comes out and gets the mail, maybe waters the garden if it's hot enough. Sometimes I can see her through the window, but I don't really watch her like that. I just sit in my chair and she comes out and gets the mail. And sometimes we smile at each other. But that's it.'

This is what I tell Ward. We're sitting drinking coffee and it's raining outside. Inside it's the hiss and spit of the hot-plate, the waitress with a dead front tooth and the council workers eating beans and toast on a wet Monday morning. We're sitting in a corner booth and I tell Ward about the girl, about how every day she's there. Then yesterday she wasn't, and today she wasn't either. I tell him about Trent Detroit; how she was Trent Detroit's girl.

'Corea,' Ward says, dropping his voice a little, 'Corea, who the hell is Trent Detroit?' You tend to drop your voice when talking about things around here, because this is where, just a few months ago, whores stood the corners like they were street signs; this is where guys like Detroit live in trust homes on a government allowance while they're making a bundle selling heroin to kids with no teeth. I've lived in Wingfield all my life and I know that when a guy like Detroit sets a girl up in a house like that so his wife doesn't get bugged, and that girl just ups and disappears like she did yesterday, then I know everything's not straight. And this is roughly what I tell Ward.

Detroit

The blood's sprayed across the window and anyone can tell you that's not a good thing. Pip's sitting watching the TV like it's all that's going on here, and Clarence is trying to find this guy's hand.

Is it One For The Road, John?

I look at the TV and there's a cartoon of a guy walking down a road. 'Clarence,' I say. I try and see where Clarence is but can't. I say, 'Clarence, have you found it, what fuck?'

'Yeah, I've got it.' He walks in from the kitchen and he's holding a cereal packet with ice spilling out the top. 'It was under the table.'

He looks at the TV, then at me. He shakes the box. 'I've put it on ice,' he says. He shakes the box again and an ice cube drops onto the carpet. He looks at the guy who's got an old soiled tea-towel wrapped round his arm. I'd given him the towel and told him to get the hell out. But then we couldn't find his hand so he's been standing here getting blood on the carpet while Clarence looked for it.

Dead End? the TV says.

There's a knock at the door.

'Road to nowhere,' Pip says. She's staring all fever-eyed at the TV.

Is it A Road to Nowhere?

There's applause and Pip looks at me and says, 'I got it, Trent.' She smiles, 'I got it,' and her eyes are all thick and fevered.

There's another knock on the door, and this time it really registers. There's blood on the window, a guy with a dripping red towel round his arm and Clarence standing with a cereal box with blood starting to fall in deep red drops from the bottom. And there's a knock on the door.

Ward

So Corea tells me about Trent Detroit. That he's a guy who lives in a trust home on a government allowance while he makes a bundle selling heroin to kids on the street. Now I know Corea, and I know he probably didn't sleep one bit last night. He's got patches of stubble growing along his jaw line, thickening a bit below the chin, and he keeps rubbing at this stubble on his chin, stroking and rubbing, knotting his brow between sentences. Corea's a decent kid and I know he's taken this on like it was his girl. Thing is, she's only been gone since yesterday. Highly likely she's just with Detroit while the guy's wife is away. That's what I tell Corea. And I tell him that all the time we've been coming to this greasy spoon, he hasn't spoken once about this girl. And I say it's a little strange that he's talking like he's gone fallen for this girl who he can't even see anymore. I tell him that's a little strange.

'I suppose I could go and see Detroit,' he says. 'Ask him where's the girl.'

'You know this guy? I mean, you can just go round there and ask like that?'

'Yeah, I can ask like that. I know the guy.' Corea finishes his coffee. He's staring beyond me now but when I turn to follow his gaze all I can see is the dirty grey street outside.

'He came to see me when he moved the girl in there. My brother used to score off him before he shot his brain on base. I haven't seen Detroit a whole lot since my brother fucked up, but I still know the guy.' He goes to sip his coffee, forgetting it's empty. 'I could go see him,' he says.

Corea

'Shit, Corea, even if you tried you couldn't have caught me at a worse time.'

'Sorry,' I say. Then I add, 'but I didn't try.' This is to reassure him. All this blood makes me want to reassure him of everything.

There's blood on the floor and the window, and on the towel that's wrapped around a guy's hand and the guy's just standing, smiling, in the middle of the lounge room, dripping blood on the carpet.

'What happened,' he tells me, 'is this guy knew I was selling, so he comes in here with that little pistol you see over there by the phone. I'm here watching TV with my wife and my boy Clarence, and this guy comes in with that pistol trying to lift me of my gear. Thing is, Clarence has a gun just like that. Thing is, see, this guy – his gun's not real. It's a replica and my boy calls it like that, because he's got one just like it. So I knock the guy one and pin him. And I tell Clarence to go fetch my axe – one of those half-handled jobs, the hatchet-types you get from hardware stores – and I take off the guy's hand. I got him a towel and told him to get the hell out; problem was in all the excitement we couldn't find his damn hand until just now. And that's when you knocked.'

I nod. I look at his wife watching TV on the couch and I smile real politely at her. Then I smile at the kid, Clarence, who's holding a packet of cereal.

'The hand's in there,' Detroit says to me. I nod again.

* * *

After speaking to Ward, I had gone home to sit in my deck chair. The rain had stopped and the sun was out. There was a small puddle of water on the chair that I mopped up with my handkerchief. I sat down and looked across at the house opposite. The Down's syndrome boy from the corner came by and put some leaflets in the girl's letterbox. He smiled at me and I waved. When he had gone I watched the girl's door to see if she'd come out to check the mail or maybe just look up and down the street like she sometimes did. But the door never even looked like it was going to open. Finally I got up and went and had a look through her window. I could see some of her clothes and underwear. The TV and everything else was still there, so it wasn't like she'd moved out or anything. I went around the back, squeezing between the wall and corrugated iron fence, almost burning myself on the water heater that stood tall and hot by the side of the house. I could feel it heating my clothes as I pressed past. My jeans were still a little wet from the rain and they rubbed all warm and moist, all uncomfortable against my leg. Around back there was no grass or flowers or anything, just damp steaming earth and tufts of yellowing weed. I looked through the windows, then decided to go see Detroit.

* * *

So now I'm here and I wish I wasn't. Detroit asks me what I want, and I turn from Clarence to him, then to the guy getting blood all over the carpet. I turn back to Detroit. 'Can we talk in the kitchen?' I ask.

In the kitchen I tell Detroit about the girl; about how I think maybe something's happened to her. And he begins smiling. His lips peel back and a set of dark teeth just spread out across his face and he's smiling.

'Corea,' he says and leads me down the hallway, away from the kitchen and the lounge room. It's a little colder back here and I can only just hear the TV, trailing like some half-memory behind me.

'You wanna see her?' asks Detroit. 'She's in here,' he nods towards the room we're standing in front of. 'You wanna see her ...' he enquires again, opening the door and letting it creak an inch or two, 'then shit, man, she's in here.'

Now he swings the door right open and walks in. I stand in the frame and try to make things out in the darkness. I don't really want to go into the dark like that with Detroit. Something drops onto the carpet and Detroit curses and switches on a lamp in the room's corner. I see the girl lying on the bed. I can really only see her bare legs from here, one of the knees sticking up oddly in the air. But I can see it's her. I step back a little, still watching.

'What're you doing just standing there?' Detroit asks. He's near me now, leaning against the doorframe, obscuring my view of the girl. 'You know,' he says, 'if you wanna be left alone for a while,' he's brought his face real close to mine now and his breath is hitting me all moist and sour, 'then that's okay.'

'Is she ..?'

'Shit, Corea, she's just a little smacked out is all.' He turns and looks at the girl and I notice her legs twitching a little. 'She's just fine.'

He begins walking back towards the kitchen. I look from him to the girl, then back to him. The TV's a little louder now and I can hear Detroit's wife yelling something. I look once more at the girl, then follow Detroit into the kitchen.

'You know,' I say, having trouble with the words, 'that's okay. As long as she's okay then that's fine. Really.' I walk past him into the lounge, where Clarence and his mother are watching television.

'Over the top,' shouts the mother, not taking her eyes off the television. I rush out the front door without saying goodbye to any of them. It's cold and getting dark. I look down the street to where the guy with the bloodied towel is hobbling across a quiet intersection. Beneath his arm is the cereal box. I hear Detroit's front door open but don't turn to look. Instead, I walk away from the house and the man with the cereal box; I walk away from that and towards the dark, swollen clouds that sit like bruised limbs ahead of me.

Jennifer Lusk

Safe-Haven

You are my harbour in the storm,
    You are my light when all is bleak
And in my night, you keep me warm.

Should the spirits try to deform
    My life, and mental havoc wreak,
You'll be my harbour in the storm.

You are the one who can transform
    My broken heart and tear stained cheek
For in my night you keep me warm.

And when the screaming faces swarm
    And my voice is too small to speak
You are my harbour in the storm.

I know my manner's not the norm
    And often less than mild and meek
But in my night you keep me warm.

When I, at last, wish to reform
    My bruised and aching soul, I'll seek
You out, my harbour in the storm
And in my night you'll keep me warm.

Dusk

S he sat upon the hill, blonde hair blowing in the growing wind. Her grey eyes gazed out across the city, watching the sun sink into the sea on the distant horizon. She scoffed at the almost corny perfection of the evening as she pulled her rough wool coat tight around her. It was growing cold and dark, almost as if the gods knew what was to come. She breathed deeply, taking in the scent of cut grass and expectant rain and then sighed. He would be here soon. It was almost time.

She heard his footsteps before she saw him, heard the soft crackle of shoes on dead leaves. She caught the smell of his aftershave. It was *brut*, cheap. The same smell clung to her own clothes, had settled in her room. She did not turn, but instead maintained her steady study of the city lights.

'Leah?' His voice was soft, plaintive. She closed her eyes against the emotion it evoked. She did not want to be emotional. She wanted to maintain control.

'Have a seat, Bobby.' He sat beside her, too close. She could feel the warmth emanating from him; smell the sweat that the steep climb up the hill had created. She put her hand in her lap so he could not take it and willed him to move away. He did not.

'Leah, look at me.' She bowed her head, fighting anger, pain, love. He was so close to her, his breath pushing against her cheek as he sought to see in under the mask of hair. She snapped her head up, forcing him back and turned to face him.

His eyes were brown, deep, full of confusion and worry. He did not understand, did not understand what was happening to them. His perfect elliptical eyes, blind to the obvious truth, wide open, but closed to reality. His mouth hung open in surprise, an unformed question desperately trying to escape his lips. She reached up and placed a finger against them, silencing them. The blood pulsed under her touch, hot against her freezing fingers. He reached his own hand up to her face, cupping her cheek before she could stop him. His callused hands were rough on her face, warm on her skin. He had always had warm hands, gentle, kind. He leant in and kissed her, wet, salty with sweat, warm and peppermint.

She pushed him away. 'Don't,' she said softly.

'Why?' he asked, his brow creasing in frustration. 'What is it? Why are we here? We only come here when … It's too cold to … ' a slow blush spread across his stubbled face. 'Why did you ask me to meet you here?'

She knew he knew, deep inside, in the paranoid places he desperately tried to silence. She knew he understood. Even this naïve man was not that innocent, that blind. He had felt her coolness, her growing distance from him. She looked at him, seeking out that suspicion that suppressed knowledge. She watched his face drop in comprehension, the jaw hang low, the breath rush from his lungs, the colour from his cheeks.

'Why?' he asked.

She had been expecting this question, anticipating it, dreading it. She herself did not exactly know. She looked up at the clouded sky, pushing her hair from her face, soft and silky between her fingers. The wind was cold and damp against her face and her nose tingled in the chill air. She sniffed, hating herself for it, not wanting the sound to be mistaken for weeping. She had no tears to cry this night. She stood and he grabbed her hand.

'Why?' he asked again, louder, more insistently.

The sky rumbled, impatient for an answer. She braced herself as she wrenched her hand from his grasp.

'Because I don't love you anymore,' she whispered.

Without looking down she turned as lightening broke the night. She walked away, leaving him shattered beneath the weeping sky, his tears mingling with the rain. She left him there, on the hill with the view, where they had first made love so long ago under a night of endless stars.

Soul Searching

The finger of flame has turned upon itself,
And I'm more than willing to offer myself.
Do you want my presence or need my help?
Who knows where that might lead?

Crowded House, *Fall At Your Feet*

You clung to her when she arrived, couldn't leave her side. She was so beautiful, the picture of elegance. You kept making excuses to touch her, hoping she wouldn't notice. Or that she would but wouldn't mind. Then you cursed yourself when you saw the look of distaste flash in her eyes. She knew, she minded. You made an effort at small talk, at friendly conversation, but your voice was heavy with rejection and she wasn't interested. She was only interested in him.

You watched her for the rest of the night, watched her make an arse of herself. Your eyes were on her as she threw herself at him, at the man you hated. You hated him because he was your antithesis, because his every action, thought, reason went against your morality, your sense of honour. You hated him because he had her, but mostly you hated him because he hurt her. So many times he had made her pretty little face contort and twist and her eyes flood with tears, tears you wiped away. And you hated her for running back to him, for wanting him, for throwing herself at him when he so obviously didn't care.

The song played and the lines touched you, reached into your heart and pulled. You thought of her as the words drifted, floated between you. How you wanted to tell her, to have her see what the words really meant, how they were written just for the two of you. But you couldn't tell her and you couldn't be there, so close, so far. You said nothing as you left, but you paused outside the doorway just long enough to hear her laugh at you. Her laugh was uncertain, stemming from her own pain and insecurity, but it hurt like hell, like a knife in your heart. It pushed you halfway down the driveway before they dragged you back inside saying, 'Don't worry about it. What does she matter?'

She's everything, your heart screamed but you said nothing; just let their ineffective words of comfort wash over you as you sank into the sofa.

Later you watched her leave. You hugged her goodbye and then stood by and watched as she loaded him, drunk, into her car. You wanted to grab her, slap her, tell her to wake up, scream at her. You wanted her to see her mistake before she made it. You smiled softly, cursing your weakness and clung to her words, 'I'll be back in half an hour.' You went inside and sat amongst the drunkards. You wallowed in your misery and waited for her to come back.

She didn't.

You hated her that weekend, you told yourself you were through with her, that you no longer cared. You turned off your heart after she had ripped it from you and you placed it back in your chest dead and unfeeling. She had pushed you away for the last time. She was on her own now. You would not wipe away her tears again. You would not pick up her pieces again. You would no longer offer your soul up to an uncaring bitch.

But then she came to you eyes wide and full of tears again. Your heart thawed and the silence in your chest was broken by the tick, tick, tick of your love. You needed her again, but not like before. You were changed, stronger and she was weaker. You had more control, more strength, more power and it was important, though you might never use it. You were still uncertain but one thing was sure. You loved her.

* * *

You had thought to yourself, maybe. Now that you were alone, maybe. Maybe if you just tried, you could be what he wanted you to be. But when you arrived, you had no eyes for him, only the other, the one who had hurt you, destroyed you, the one you still wanted so badly. You could see only the other, and the friend you loved and cherished was pushed aside.

You saw him watching you; saw him judging you. You loved him and thanked him for caring, but you just wanted to be left alone, to be free to pursue your desires. You had no commitment to him, so why did you feel so guilty? You tried to forget your guilt in vodka and wine, but it still nagged at you. You ignored him, stepped up your pursuit of the other, but still something was eating at you. You told yourself you didn't care.

You did.

You saw him leave the room and told yourself it wasn't your fault, that you were not obligated to cocoon his feelings, that you were not to blame. You never believed it.

And then you betrayed him. You left with the other, the one he hated so much it hurt. Hurt you in an overflow of pain. You told him you would be back. You weren't lying. You honestly believed you would be strong enough to resist, to pull away. You hugged him goodbye and left with no intention of betraying him, for as much as his attention annoyed you, you did love him. You weren't lying. You were coming back.

But then you found yourself in that small apartment with temptation dangling before you. You went back the way you had come; down a path you already knew to be full of pain and tears. The carrot before your nose was too much. You had to know, had to try one last time and hope it wouldn't end in the same way. You had to try and pray that you wouldn't have to run back to him crying, ashamed and proven wrong.

Why did you have to need them both so much, but each in the wrong way?

You woke up in the middle of the night from a half sleep, cold and numb with the realisation that you had been fooled. Again. You stumbled from the apartment and drove home in a tear-blinded daze. You cried yourself to sleep.

You hated yourself that weekend. You hated yourself for being weak, for making the same mistake twice, for being a fool. But mostly you hated yourself for hurting him, for betraying him. You heard the song, those words that had driven him from the room, and it hit you, the true nature of his love. The added guilt was all consuming as you began to understand. You spent the weekend crying, loathing yourself, and sat motionless, like a shell filled with salt.

When you saw him, you cried again. You saw the pain you had caused him written on his face and the guilt came in waves of tears. You realised then just how much you needed him. You needed his love, needed his forgiveness. He gave it readily and you could begin to forgive yourself. He seemed different. Stronger, more in control, while you were weak, a wreck of the self you were before. You would recover, but you needed help, needed him. You loved him.

*   *   *

Your love went unspoken, changed but not recognised. Until a night, filled with stars and jazz, waves and moonlight. A night made for lovers. You walked hand in hand down a jetty strewn with lazy couples enjoying the romance. You were awkward and excited and so terribly nervous. You were uncertain, almost sick with fear. You stopped and you both knew it could not be avoided, both knew there was no going back. Neither of you were the type to be tested by a toe dipped in the pool. No, this was a headlong dive into dark waters, inviting but terrifying. You stood, huddled into each other against the wind. You looked over the edge into the unknown.

And then, hand in hand, you jumped.

The kiss was strange, new, different. It was an exploration, a search for a new connection, a building of a new love.

It was a start.

You pulled away from each other, less afraid but still unsure. But your uncertainty came, not from nervous anticipation, but from the knowledge that there truly was no going back. Your new love was named, declared and would not be silenced. You looked into each other's eyes and comforted the other with soft smiles. You moved together again, becoming another faceless pair of lovers on the jetty.

And you both knew then that it would all be all right, that you had found peace and safety in each other, found yourselves. You realised that for so long you had been looking in the wrong places, in the wrong people. But it didn't matter anymore because, there on that jetty, you were suddenly looking in the right place. And there, in each other's arms, you found happiness.

Twenty Minutes

'Yes, Papa ... No, Papa ... No, Papa ... Yes ... Yes ... I'll be home later ... But Papa ... Meet Tony at the airport ... ? But ... I ... Yes, Papa, twenty minutes. Goodbye, Papa.' I press the little blue button, ending the call. I put the phone on silent, wishing there were a similar button on my Papa, and place it on the table.

Twenty minutes.

'You have to leave?' he asks me, as he paces nervously around the tiny room.

'Twenty minutes.' I bite my lip and watch him as he walks, then hold out my hand to him. 'Sit, stop pacing, you're making me nervous.' He continues to pace for a few seconds, hand tapping on his jaw, eyes staring into mine. Then he stops and joins me on the couch. His feet still tap and as I place my arm around his shoulders, I feel he is shaking.

'Hey, sweetie, it's all right.' I stroke his hair, slightly damp with sweat. 'They won't find you. Not here. Remember? I chose this place so carefully. Only you and I know you're here. You don't have to be afraid anymore. You're safe.'

He leans into me, his head on my shoulder, my cheek nuzzling his black hair, sparsely dotted with grey. I can feel that he is beginning to calm down. His neck is relaxing and the weight of his head is growing. 'You're right,' he says. 'How would they find me?'

'They can't.' I kiss the top of his ear. He has such little ears, small and round and smooth.

He lifts my wrist and looks at my watch. 'Seventeen minutes.'

He turns in my arms to face me. My fingers automatically begin to twist themselves in his hair. It is so soft, like silk. He looks at me with his big, beautiful blue eyes, framed with long, thick lashes. His pupils are wide. My hand moves round to cup his cheek. He hasn't shaved today and his face is stubbled and rough. In a way, I like it better like this. It is more stimulating, more real, so different from my own soft face. My thumb moves to his lips. His breath is warm on my skin. He kisses it softly, gently. His lips are full, pink, soft. I have to kiss them. So we kiss, so gently. Usually we kiss with passion, with force, as though we have to have as much of each other as possible. This time we savour the experience. Perhaps he is afraid that this is the last time. It is like nothing else.

Bittersweet.

We pull away and I look at my watch. 'Fourteen minutes.'

'It's not enough.'

'I know.'

I'm leaving tonight, with my father. I don't want to go, but he says I have to. He doesn't trust me, perhaps with good reason. Me? I'd rather stay in this tiny little flat in the middle of nowhere than fly to Chicago with Papa. I won't even see Papa. It is a business trip, a family thing. I love Papa, very dearly, but he doesn't understand me. He didn't understand Mama either and he still doesn't understand why she left. She didn't like his rules, didn't want me raised to follow them, believe in them. I have different rules to Papa, but ever since Mama died, I've had to forget them, live my life his way. I hate his rules.

Thirteen minutes.

He sighs, 'When are you coming back?'

'I don't know.'

'Are you coming back?'

That shocks me. I hold his neck in one hand and his arm in the other and look deep into his eyes so he cannot doubt my words. I speak slowly and clearly. 'Even if Papa never comes back, I will. I will do anything I can to get back here. I don't want to disobey Papa, God knows I've done that enough already, but if I have to I will. Even if it means I never see Papa again.'

He tries to argue. I place a finger across his lips. 'I know what that would mean. I know the dangers of going against Papa. I don't care. If I cared I wouldn't be here now, would I?'

He smiles weakly. His arm is tense, the muscle raised. I look at his hand. It is clenched tightly, the knuckles almost white. I move my own hand down to it and worm my fingers into his, forcing him to relax. His hands are dry, but soft. His fingers are long and the knuckles slightly twisted. He begins to play with my fingers, an automatic reaction.

'I'm so scared,' he says, 'that I will never see you again.'

'You will see me again. I promise.'

'I know, but there's just something … Like the feeling you get after a nightmare. This ball in the pit of my stomach,' he takes my hand and places it on the spot, 'telling me that this is it. This is the end.'

'Don't say that. Please.' I watch as a tear traces its way down his cheek and one threatens to do the same to mine. Despite my fear and sadness I laugh, trying to shake it off.

'You're just being silly!' He smiles. Such a beautiful smile. His cheeks crinkle into dimples and the laugh lines under his eyes fold into their customary wrinkles. He thinks they make him look old. I think they make him look happy.

Six minutes.

I kiss him again. More passionately this time. I explore his mouth, his lips, his tongue, his teeth. I don't ever want to forget what it is like to kiss him. I want to be able to bring this to mind every night that we are separated. My hands trace their way down his back, feeling each muscle beneath his shirt, beneath my palms. I breathe in deeply, capturing the slightly spicy smell that is always lingering on his clothes, his face, his hair. I love that smell. It is what first drew me to him. I never want to forget that smell.

We pull away.

Three minutes.

I get up and move to the door. He opens it for me and I step out onto the dimly lit landing and look down the steep steps that will lead me from my love. I turn to him. He is framed in the doorway by the light from the apartment, like an angel. My angel. He slips his arms around my waist.

'Call me.'

'You know I can't.'

'I know.'

Two minutes.

'I'll be back soon.' I wipe the tear from his cheek. 'I promise.'

He looks at me with eyes full of sadness and loss and kisses me one last time. I hold him for what seems like an eternity but it is still not long enough. Then I move down the narrow stairs and listen for the awful sound of the door closing behind him. Such finality. I turn the corner and run into a man. He is dressed in black, large and imposing. I begin to apologise but as I look up, I recognise him. Images flash of drawing room meetings and closed doors, of handshakes and condescending smiles. I don't know his name but I've known him my whole life. He looks at me with hard, black eyes. His jaw grinds and there is an unspoken message in his face. Go, he is telling me. Run and don't look back. Then he moves up the stairs and I walk out the screen door into the cold winter air. I am crying by the time I get to the car.

Time's up.

I rev the engine as the clock runs out. The sudden noise of the radio and the car muffles the single shot. I drive away, singing to some stupid song with tears streaming down my face, not even bothering to look in the rear-view mirror.

Catherine Bown

Laugh long and loud

Too often spoken yet never sung.
    I wish I'd proclaimed joy from the rooftops.

Too often dreamed and not made real.
    I wish I'd pursued life more passionately.

Too often deliberated but not prayed over.
    I wish I'd prayed deliberately.

Too often (too much time) spent at my computer.
    I wish I'd danced outside with butterflies.

Too often internally processed as an inner thought.
    Why didn't I summon my courage and vocalise?

Too often pitied and discarded as a bench warmer.
    Why didn't I remember that you're more than the
        twelfth man?

Too often spent being serious, solemn and stern.
    Why didn't I laugh long and loud? (Like a lout)

Too often I drove my automobile to work
    Why didn't I hike to the office despite typhoon or
        drought?

Too often debated, argued and reasoned by my ego.
    I'd like to have abandoned my narcissism.

Too often my jaw has been set with knives and my teeth
        as swords.
    I'd like to have spoken words of milk and honey.

Too often fasted, refused and refrained from.
  I'd like to have drunk fast and furiously.

Too often in front of the mirror
  I'd like to have smashed it to pieces.

Too often tangled upside-down in my fears.
  Now I would have ripped the web apart.

Too often I worried about the threat of rain.
  Now I would caper through puddles and gutters.

Too often I patronised and simplified you.
  Now I would extol your youthful outlook.

Too often I ate chocolate, saturated fats and oils.
  Now I would … do exactly the same!

Pinpricked Stars

You haunt my dreams
I wake drunk on your image.
The next day I'm hung-over:
Recovering as my dream replays.

At nightfall we ride to nowhere,
Beefy motorbikes beneath us,
Talk with locals in that town
Laughing and gossiping too.

And we stop on the way home
Sprawling out on grass beneath stars
Littering the sky with pinpricks.
They dance and so we dance too.

Limbs chaotic and spread out
Like demented stars unravelling.

Rolling down the grassy paddock
I feel sick and so alive.

I replay the scene, then rewind
To the part where you drink me in.
It's you and me with pinpricked stars.
Do you want to fly away?

'Pigs might fly … and I'm that,' you cry.
We kill ourselves with laughter.
It rides on and over valleys
With our beefy motorbikes.

I press pause and drink in your face
Every feature permeating
Me and the smell of your neck,
This scent lingers on and on.

The night zips forwards and back,
Then the dream aborts itself.
And I'm stranded without you,
Hung-over as my dream replays.

Spit

Claire feels like a yellow daffodil
Dancing on a green sea of grass.
He's said that he's in love with her
And she believes him, poor darling.

Time passes and she adores him
The honeymoon is sugar sweet.
Feasting on each other, she swoons.
He is her life and salvation.

Claire feels like spiced apple-blossom
Mixed with honeyed milk and stirred well.

He's said his work is too urgent
And she believes him, poor darling.

Another night alone in bed
Claire won't cry but she holds her doll.
Lucy only has one eye and
Claire's balloon of pain finally bursts.

Claire feels like an exposed cactus,
Jagged and barren in her grief.
He's said it's her fault they've no spawn
And she believes him, poor darling.

In a few dozen weeks and months
It will be jaded and hollow.
She'll throb and sob and wail and scream
Accusations as lovers do.

Claire feels like purple bougainvillea
Clinging limply to barbed wire.
He rages threats of brutality
And she believes him, poor darling.

Deflowered and disgraced she leaves
With stomach in and head held high.
She epitomises success
And spitting is her last remark.

Will you be my umpire?

And she talked as she sipped,
Gazing into her glass
(Naturally chocolate milkshake for my sister).

She did nod as she watched,
Our mother wave her hands
(Normally vanilla milkshake for my mother).

And I sat in between,
With my pineapple juice
Like an umpire at his first grand-final match.

And I looked at them both,
Then one, then the other.
There were tears and jokes and silences and straws.

And we were the three women who shared it.

Yesterday, Today and Tomorrow

Today I hiccupped my way through life.
Asked to give snippets of counsel
– That I failed to follow myself –
So I fell in the pit I warned against,
And was alone due to my wise advice.

Today I yawned my way through life.
And it made it difficult to talk
– Which is what I think I do best –
So I was frustrated and felt all day
Particularly silent and unheard.

Today I blinked my way though life.
I think I had my eyes closed
– More than opened –
Life rolled by, scene by scene, without me.
I felt like a famous director!

Today I farted my way through life.
Habitually excreting opinions
– A pungent smell –
To any individual who challenged
My thoughts with logic or reason.

Today I winked my way through life.
And desperately tried to avoid eye contact
– She always talks for hours on hours –
Besides I'm on a tight schedule.
No room for improvisation.

Today I flared my nose at life.
I think I am getting the flu
– And I tried not to look like a horse –
Stamping my feet in the cold snow
But every winter it comes and I sniffle.

Today I poked my tongue out at life.
Clowning around I erred and fell
– Metaphorically on a banana peel –
Rather humiliating but funny
So I reluctantly laughed at myself.

Today I burped my way through life.
My red-hot temper erupted
– I got myself into a girl-fight –
And my sudden response had the aftertaste
Of this morning's breakfast in my throat.

Today I whistled through life.
An off-key tune weaving through octaves
– By means of quavers and semitones –
Do only old men whistle when they walk?
Well not any more: I've joined their ranks!

Stuart Jones

Galactic Census 2001

The Galactic Census has been a part of the Order for almost 200 years. When it first started, the New Government had just been formed, joining the ruling councils from six neighbouring systems and our council, from my home planet of Trasis in the Besta system.

This mega council, while finding the merger great for trade and the sharing of information, found it difficult to dispatch resources to areas that needed it the most. So the census was born.

Each system was assigned a caretaker and was monitored for any needs. Also, each year all citizens would participate in the census to give the New Government a better idea of the situations of all areas.

After the first 100 years the census became unnecessary, as the government had enough data to predict movement within the systems and enough resources to supply all areas with more than enough.

There was talk of scraping the census entirely, but the government decided that the information would still be useful, if only for historic or educational value.

Soon after that, the government began its first deep space research missions and, in an act of true brilliance, decided to tie in the research with the existing census system. Each year a growing number of newly located worlds would be surveyed and added to the existing database, which quickly became the most comprehensive listing of the planets and systems in the galaxy.

Last year the last of the inhabitable worlds were added to the database, making it the only complete list in existence. And this year every world in the listing will undergo the census, bringing the information up-to-date for all areas of the galaxy.

I have worked for the census bureau for five years, carefully collating information from the many missions to the inhabited worlds of the galaxy. This year I have been given a job that, as my superior puts it, 'after last year, fits your expertise precisely.' I now drain and replace the coolant for the computer system that houses the census information. It's a dirty job, but someone has to do it. The computer is extremely important to the government, it calculates and reports anything that is required.

Last year I had the privilege of undertaking the census for the third planet of the Sol system, a small blue-green planet known by the inhabitants as 'Earth'. Earth is still classified as 'Pre-Contact,' so the census had to be carried out by an undercover observer.

Namely ... me.

*   *   *

As the steam dissipated, I stepped out of the transportation along with the other passengers. I had done some preliminary research to make sure I would blend into the society, however there seemed to be some inconsistencies with my data. The transport was as I expected, but the clothing of the people was remarkably different.

I decided to find out what was going on from the one man that *was* dressed as I expected, in blue jacket and pants, cap and whistle. He was the controller of the transport, I believe.

'Hello,' he said as I approached him. 'I don't remember seeing you get aboard, were you on for the whole trip?'

'Well, no, I uh ... '

'You must have come on with that big group from the other end then?'

'Well, I urgh ... '

'Thought so. It gets pretty hectic at the other end of the line sometimes, I must have just forgotten you.'

'Yes,' I replied.

'But let me just say, I *love* your outfit, and the luggage! It's just *great* to see someone really getting into the sprit of the trip. I bet that *no one* has taken luggage aboard the train since it was taken out of service fifty years ago.'

'Out of service?'

'Yes. What, didn't you know this was the real thing? It's not some replica, like they've got back where *you* come from, you've been travelling in a genuine steam train.'

'No doubt, no doubt.' I replied.

'What is that accent anyway?'

'Excuse me?'

'Where are you from? France?'

'Um, no, urgh ... Scandinavia.'

'Ah ... yep ... yeah, I *thought* I recognised the inflection.'

I quickly stepped aside for a little family who were trying to get a photo with the controller, and began my journey to the hotel where I would be staying.

As I walked through the town I saw many things that puzzled me. It wasn't as if I have never seen such strange people or advanced technology, but these people had changed dramatically in the few years that had passed between the initial survey probe and my visit last year.

As I crossed over a road, I noticed a woman with an exceptionally brilliant head of blue hair. There was no report of such a colour occurring naturally on people's heads. I was determined to find out what had happened, so I approached the lady in question.

'Is that a natural occurrence?' I asked, motioning toward her hair.

'Sure mate, yeah, it's natural,' she replied. I must admit that I was surprised, but I noted it down and moved on.

I soon found the hotel that I was to book in to, but it seemed to have been converted into some sort of medical facility. I didn't know this at first, however, and the girl at the desk was quite shocked when I asked if I could book a room with a view over the town centre, for two weeks.

The misunderstanding was soon cleared after a talk with man named Security, who introduced me to some men in white. They offered me a nice white jacket, but I had to decline because of a fault with the arms.

I finally found an actual hotel and successfully managed to get a room that had quite a good view across the park nearby. When the attendant had left me to settle in my room, I began to unpack my suitcase, carefully laying out all of my possessions on the bed.

When the survey probe had come back from Earth, just short of eighty years ago, the scientists began to create what I was now pulling out of my suitcase. It was found long ago, on a mission to another planet, that the people of a world would accept a person easier if they had all the belongings that normal people had in their world.

In an attempt to find out a little more information about the town I was in, I decided to go down stairs and ask some questions. The man at the front desk was very talkative and I learned many facts about the town, which would help me a lot, and even more about his life story. While I was there I offered to pay for my first week, but when the man saw my money he nearly fell off of his chair.

'What are you trying to do with that? You can't buy anything with pounds, that's over fifty years old that money. We've changed the currency you know. You must have been ripped off before you left your country. Where are you from anyway? France?'

'No, no,' I said. 'Scandinavia.'

'Ah yeah, I've been there many times myself. It's beautiful at this time of year.'

'Sure is,' I agreed.

'Well, with that money you could go to the coin and stamp shop down the road there.'

'Yeah?'

'They might buy your old coins, and you'll probably find that they're worth more than the currency is now, the dollar being so low and all. You'll almost certainly come out a lot better than you are now.'

'Indubitably.' I thanked him profusely and, after looking at his photo album and experiencing in detail the births of his ten children, I staggered back to my room.

After resting a moment. I picked some clothes off my bed that seemed to fit in a little better with what the people were wearing at the time; I gave the waistcoat a miss, left the shirt untucked, and strapped the fob watch to my wrist with an adhesive strip from a nearby dispenser.

I then began an exhausting week of being unbearably nosey.

I'd go to a shopping centre and look in people's trolleys. I'd take a ride on a bus and get involved in other people's conversations. If I saw something in a shop that I didn't know about, I would ask the staff hundreds of questions. All this had to be done so I could become an authority on all things Earthly.

I soon became tired of being so intrusive though, and, after being almost slapped across the face by a woman for asking her about her particular brand of perfume, I was ready to give up. I really thought that her perfume was a cheap substitute for the real thing but, from her reaction, I was obviously wrong.

I sat in my hotel room that night, instead of going out as usual, and wished I didn't have to be such a bother to people.

Like a messenger from the stars, the concierge's assistant knocked on the door to see if I needed anything.

'No, I'm fine,' I replied, staring out of the window.

'Are you sure? You look a bit bored, is your TV working?'

'My what?' I looked around and the assistant motioned toward a cupboard in the corner.

'It's in here, don't tell me they don't have TVs where you come from?' he asked as he opened the cupboard doors.

'Of course they do,' I said, trying to be convincing as I looked at the controls on the side of the box.

'Where are you from anyway?'

'Umm ... I'm from France.'

'Huh. I could have sworn that was more of a Scandinavian accent ... Well have fun with the TV. I don't know if there's anything good on tonight, but there's a few videos that you can borrow, down in the room at the end of the hall, OK?'

'Sure,' I said, 'thanks.'

I began to look at the various channels available on the TV and, after watching a few things, I began to understand much more about Earth.

There's no need to go walking the streets of this town to find out about Earth, I said to myself. *This TV will provide me with more information than I could possibly find out in two weeks of being nosey.*

By the end of my second week I had documented more information about Earth with the television than I did in the first week walking around town. It was plain to me now that the wrong town had been chosen for any study of humanity. The lives of the people documented on television were much more exiting than those I had met. Many interesting things were learned from that television. For instance, I found out that humans had actually contacted many species of life from other worlds. They had been travelling around the stars for many years with ships that could travel faster than light and they were using laser-like weapons that were far superior to our own.

I was ready to pack up, go back to Trasis, and recommend immediate contact with Earth, in order for our government to join their planetary alliance.

And that's exactly what I did.

* * *

I had no idea that what I saw on television was a fabrication, and neither did my superiors, until a delegation from the government went to Earth in order to approach the leaders of the alliance and found that none existed. They looked into the information I received from the television and found that it was all a production. Something made for entertainment, and worse, something that hardly anyone on Earth believed would actually happen.

I was dealt with severely, my family was dishonoured, and I was stuck draining coolant from the computer system.

At least I have one comfort in my life. I have a friend who pops by Earth every now and then, and brings me the latest episodes of *Star Trek* to play on the television and video player I brought back with me.

Annie Maynard

Diva

A battered bathtub with shuddering pipes
stands, steaming in the icy night.
Her head rests against the decaying bone
of chipped ceramic –
make-up clots in welts of clay,
simmering across her face,
black beads roll from her gory eyes
and red lipstick plunges violently down her neck.

She lolls in the dark
Swigging sapphire gin.

The audience, bestial in their adoration
Have ravaged her ears,
run hooks through her presence.
She has stood, splendid in jaundiced light
glassy, magnificent
marble breasted god of accomplished charm.
Revered, respected, rewarded
and humanised by hotel bathtubs
and slippery tonics.

She lolls in the dark
Swigging sapphire gin.

Twenty years of buxom fame,
at parties she has laughed with diamonds in her eyes,
lapped at the oyster of luxury,
trailed bleeding fishtails of silk
Now –
a grimy demise, derelict in a lonely city

She lolls in the dark
Swigging sapphire gin

… and her voice had begun to wither
to decompose in her throat.
Her composure composted
the audience inhaled its breath in shame.
Through spectacles and binoculars
the diva's wretched encore spied
in tatters.

She lolls in the dark
Swigging sapphire gin

And they have left her here –
in a rotting hotel, with a torn signature
where she lolls in the dark
Amongst wilted hair of flotsam
perception eclipsed
she swigs her sapphire gin
and slips beneath the rancid water.
Tomorrow's wretched retrospective.

Edwina Stark

3+1-2

There were three.

There's a 24-year-old woman framed by a window
and she is kissing a Peter Jackson
the chalk-white stem pressed to her lips
a thin strand slides from her mouth
       slithering and curling
              and winding round her neck;
                    a ghostly snake.

There's a 30-year-old boy throned on a canvas-backed chair
and he's sucking down a three-course cereal banquet
Rice Bubbles, Cornflakes, Coco Pops
       slurping and crunching
              gurgling; milk drenching the folds
                  of his frown.

There's a 26-year-old man strung up as a puppet by the fridge
and he can't decide on a drink
and he hesitates over a proffered bong
and he takes to the stairs to change his t-shirt.
              'Third time lucky,'
                he thinks.

Then there were four.
Four people share three chairs
and guzzle vodka from three tumblers
and gut pies with three knives
              and three forks
and coffee is drained from three mugs
              and one stein.

Number four watches *A Current Affair*
               instead of *Neighbours*.
She cooks tofu burgers
               instead of beef.
Now the 26-year-old man wears Armani
and takes Zyban with herbal tea.

They prop against the fridge
They stare at the young woman and middle-aged boy;
               they stutter
                    mutter
And the fluorescent light catches the golden band
The bright metal yawns at woman and boy;
               gapes at them
               screams at them that
the 26-year-old man is deserting them.

And then there were two.

There's a 24-year-old woman framed by a window
and she is kissing a Peter Jackson
the chalk-white stem pressed to her lips
a thin strand slides from her mouth
        slithering and curling
               and winding round her neck;
                   a ghostly snake.

There's a 30-year-old boy throned on a canvas-backed chair
and he's sucking down a three-course cereal banquet
Rice Bubbles, Cornflakes, Coco Pops
        slurping and crunching
               gurgling; milk drenching the folds
                   of his frown.

There's a 26-year-old man strung up as a puppet by his wife
and she makes him sip orange juice
and she stubs out his joint
and she banishes him to the bedroom to change his shirt.
            'Third time lucky,'
                 she thinks.

Breakfast with the Burtenshaws

Alexis

I burn my tongue on my Milo. It is so hot, I spit it out, some of it dribbling down my school jumper in long, milky tears. I watch them soak into the brown wool, and then look up to see if anyone has noticed. Dad could be dead behind the *Advertiser* for all I know, except that I can hear him slurping his coffee. Man, it's annoying. Mum, meanwhile, is too busy trying to ignore the slurps to notice my little mishap, and Pete is, well, too busy being disgusting Pete. Checking his ugly little noggin for dandruff is obviously more important to him.

I reach for the sugar to put on my Weet-bix, but Pete snatches it away, strangely choosing to sprinkle it on his peanut butter toast. I bet Brad Pitt never acts like this when he has breakfast with Jennifer.

'Alexis, go get Grandma, would you?' Mum asks.

'But Pete could … '

'Pete's eating. I want you to go.'

This is typical. I always get lumped with this job. I stomp upstairs, my loud footsteps making it clear I am not impressed.

The sweet stench of urine stabs at my nostrils. Her rasping breath pierces my ears. I take a big gulp of air and move towards the source of the ghastly smell. I stroke her Napisan-white hair and her pale eyes open. I twist her arm around my shoulders and hoist her out of bed. Her soaked nightie sticks to my freshly dry-cleaned uniform. It sickens me, but I'm used to it and won't complain. I help her change her wrinkled body from the stained gown to a Kmart tracksuit and ease her down the stairs, into the kitchen.

In my absence Pete has replaced the sugar, leaving traces of his grotty peanut butter in it, of course. Also in my absence, my Weet-bix has turned cold and sloppy. I sigh. I bet Brad and Jennifer never have cold Weet-bix.

Joanna

I hate breakfast. My husband doesn't speak to me – and why the hell does he have to slurp like that? – my daughter is grumpy and always whinges about her Weet-bix being soggy, and the cat always throws up a fur ball in the middle of the kitchen floor. Must do something about that cat door. Lyndall could seal it up, if only he'd put down that blasted newspaper for two seconds.

As for my little Pete, what an angel. Just quietly eating his toast. Seems a little itchy, though; he keeps scratching his head.

As I mop up Pugsy's fur ball, a bitter perfume slides into my nose. Alexis is helping Grandma into her usual seat, by the oven.

'Sweetheart, did you bathe Grandma?'

'Yes,' Alexis blinks at me. I can never tell if she's lying, but the evidence is swaying me towards a guilty verdict. I let it drop. I have to get the fur ball cleaned up before Lyndall's mother comes over for a herb tea, and what I like to call a 'health inspection' of the house.

The kitchen is silent. All that can be heard is the *slop*, *slop* of the mop and my mother's dentures slipping over her Golden Circle peaches. I bet Oprah Winfrey doesn't have to clean up cat sick each morning.

Lyndall

I am worried as all buggery about the Crows. Angwin is down with a hammy and Ricciuto … Jesus, poor bloke. Can't breathe properly and no-one knows what's wrong. And why the hell did they lose to Port? Must have been a bit of dodgy umpiring going on. And the forward line. Yeah, it's the forward line, I tell ya. If I was Gary Ayers …

Jesus, what's that stink? Probably Grandma. Why doesn't Joanna do something about it? Bloody hell, I've run out of coffee. Why hasn't Joanna refilled it? Bet Gary Ayers doesn't have to put up with this sort of crap.

Pete

Got a spelling test today. Don't want to go to school. How can I get out of it? Maybe this white stuff coming out of my hair is a deadly disease. Maybe I'll get all covered in scabs and blood will come out of my eyeballs and everyone will be crying and I'll act all brave. Then Alexis will be sorry for being a cow to me. God, Nana stinks. She keeps dropping her breakfast all over herself. I hope I do have a disease and die. I don't want to end up like that. I bet Craig Lowndes doesn't have a grandma who dribbles all over herself.

Grandma

~ ~ ~ ~ ~ ~ ~ ~ ~

The Day I Wished for an Earthquake

God is a phoney. He must be. On August 11 each year, I pray for a sudden illness, a broken bone – maybe even an earthquake – but it never happens. And there's the doorbell now. My death knell.

Like a schoolgirl going to maths class, I drag my feet along the floor. Like a schoolgirl going to maths class, the dread I feel is smothering. But unlike a schoolgirl going to maths class, I would be quite content to study right now. Give me trigonometry, algebra or logarithms any day; I would gladly exchange them for dinner with my sister.

I slide back the bolt and my front door – the gate to hell – swings open, the hinges squealing in apparent horror.

'Daaaarling!' The collagen lips are outstretched towards my cheek. But I know they'll never make contact; my sister is an expert air-kisser.

Chanel (who has changed her name because 'Kate' apparently doesn't do her justice) catwalks along my hallway and moulds herself into a pose in my kitchen. Unfortunately for her, I don't think Yoko and Lennon rubbing their tabby bodies against her silk-stockinged legs is part of the performance. Chanel moves to the fridge and helps herself to a glass of cask shiraz. Its cheap taste makes her beaky nose wrinkle.

'So, my sweet, what have you been up to?' the collagen lips ask.

'Well, I've been seeing this guy and ... '

'Wooooonderful!' the lips proclaim. I could have said I was working weekends as a hitman for a little extra cash and she still would have said, 'wonderful'. Nice to know she is listening.

'As for me,' the Revlon-painted face says, 'I've been offered a position as PR Manager. It's a faaabulous opportunity for me.'

'The' is the most commonly used word in the English language; 'me' is the most commonly used word in Chanel's language.

'So, do you want some gossip?' she asks.

I figure I don't have much choice.

'Well, last week I was on holiday in Tahiti with Richard. He's just divorced a *hideous* cow. He left her for some tart he was sleeping with and I think he got engaged to her just the other day. Anyway, that relationship is doomed already – he's having an affair with me.'

My teeth clench. My eyes shrink to a painful squint. Best start using the knife in my hand to cut the carrots. So Chanel was about to break up another poor, wretched couple. No surprises there.

She continues. 'As I was saying, Richard and I were slurping down these faaabulous cocktails by the pool – did I mention I was wearing my string bikini? Anyway, we were having pina coladas, when this woman – this psychotic woman – charged toward Richard and started screaming at him. Darling, I was simply frozen to my seat.'

'Would you pass the carrots? Bottom drawer of the fridge, on the left,' I interrupt.

Chanel hunches over my stunted Panasonic fridge. She looks awkward and out of place, crouching like that.

She extends her bony claw to me, offering the carrots. 'So this crazy woman just kept shouting at Richard, calling him a bastard. Everyone was staring. Honestly, sweetie, I don't blame him for leaving her.'

'Potatoes, please,' I demand. She passes them to me. I wash them and leave them bobbing in a saucepan full of water. I feel my blood pressure rising as anger slithers through by body like poison. My heart is punching my chest. I want to call Chanel a selfish, insolent witch. I want to break her surgically reshaped nose. I want to pull her bleached hair till it is ripped out by the roots. Instead, I say, 'Pass me a spoon.'

'Here,' she replies and flexes her claw to release the utensil. Her rambling continues. 'Richard, of course, just sat there and took the abuse. I think this made his ex-wife furious because, all of a sudden, she lunged at him and bit off his … '

'Sausage,' I interrupt.

'Ear,' she says as she passes a sausage to me. I let it flop onto the greased tray and order Chanel to remove more from the fridge. I arrange the remaining sausages in a military assembly on the tray and slide them into the griller.

'Well, this woman didn't bite off his *whole* ear, just the lobe,' Chanel explains.

Her story is sickening me. Nausea is clawing at my stomach.

'And then she just clamped her hand over her mouth, like she was going to vomit or something, and ran off. Meanwhile, Richard was screaming and demanding I search for his missing ear lobe. I found it, all right, peering up at me from under the banana lounge. It still had his diamond stud protruding from it. *Eeeeeew.* He actually wanted me to pick it up and put it on ice. As if! I mean, darling, how revolting! I simply can't stand the sight of blood. How could he be so selfish?'

How, indeed.

'So he picks it up himself, with a river of blood running down his neck, and drops the lobe onto the ice in his drink, and bellows for help.'

I drain the water from the cooked potatoes as the sausages

continue to sun themselves under the griller.

'Well that just ruined my holiday. Richard's ear is a jagged mess and I got nowhere near the tan I wanted.'

The sausages hiss. My sentiments exactly, I think. The dog next door barks. The one in front of me preens her hair.

'So what did you say you'd been doing, honey?' Chanel asks as she pulls a nail file from her alligator-skin bag.

I serve the much-awaited bangers and mash and seat her at my rented table. Chanel hates it; she always says it's 'kitsch'. She flicks the food around the cracked plate. I wait until she takes a mouthful.

'Well,' I say, 'I recently got engaged to a divorced man called Richard, who has a missing ear lobe.'

Chanel spits out her sausage, splattering its guts on my wall.

The Doctor's Wife

Day One

Phil threw up on the $200 tulip bouquet next to the cheese platter. The bathroom had been a mere five staggers to his right – but his two bottles of Killawarra insisted on an escape. Sponging at his mouth with a sweaty fist, the best man stumbles back to the wedding table, a fleck of vomit in his hired shirt justifying his sudden exit. Roberta chewed her thumbnail and squeezed her new husband's hand.

Day Two

The bride couldn't wear her silver, backless dress to dinner that night, the shape of her bikini singed into her skin. Ashley kept forgetting, repeatedly wrapping an arm around her shoulders, making her flinch. The wine, waiter and Beef Wellington: 'Terrible,' said Roberta. But the Supa Sundae, spa and sex: 'Sublime,' said Ashley.

Day Sixteen

From Cairns to Sydney, Sydney to Adelaide, Roberta and Ashley nibbled on smoked salmon and one another's ears and tickled each other's business-class-slippered feet. Bored by the in-flight screening of *Braveheart*, they slipped into the toilet and made dry martinis in the stainless steel basin. Roberta and Ashley entered the cubicle composed, sober, but when the 73-year-old ex-bank manager from 3B demanded entry to relieve a bursting bladder, the naughty couple could only lurch to their seat and a disapproving hostess.

Day Seventeen

The Queen St apartment was too narrow for Roberta's grand piano. Ashley knew someone who could keep it in storage for free, which would do for now. After all, they were only going to be living there for six months, weren't they? The future surgeon would soon be able to buy a Medindie mansion, wouldn't he? The instrument was left to sulk alone, wallowing in the dust of a foreign shed.

Day Ninety-Seven

Roberta was restless, unsuccessfully scrunching about in the small army-green beanbag – the best man's wedding present – while waiting for Ashley to return from his internship at the hospital. She pined for her piano.

Ashley brought home a small electronic keyboard and plugged it in next to the radiator. Roberta played one honking note, feigned a headache and went to bed.

Day One Hundred and Twelve

When the tyres of Roberta's Laser churned up the tortoise-shell of Mandy's fur, Roberta cried and Ashley hugged her.

Day Four Hundred and Four

When Roberta crushed Tiger at 10 km/h, Ashley comforted her over the phone and blew kisses.

Day Six-Hundred and Twenty-Four
When Roberta killed cat number three, she sobbed into Ashley's Voicemail.

Day Seven Hundred and Ninety-Three
Ashley raised his eyebrow at Mr Abbott's blood pressure and encouraged him to take a holiday. It was well after 8pm when he sucked down a third brandy from the 250 mL St Agnes bottle taped to the top of his drawer. He could go home or he could catch up on his notes. Ashley poured a fourth brandy.

Roberta threw out the cold, hardened roast for two and settled on the oatmeal loveseat – alone. She sucked Cheezel crumbs off her fingers and burped out her Pale Ale.

Day Nine Hundred and Thirty-Four
Ashley volunteered to cover Dr van den Berg's Saturday morning shift and prescribed a month's supply of Ventolin for Mr Crittenden's asthma.

Roberta tired of drinking Nescafe alone and visited her next-door neighbour.

Day One Thousand and Fifty-One
Mr Simpson dropped his knee-high varicose vein support-hose on Ashley's surgery floor and climbed onto the medical examination table.

Roberta dropped her lycra pantyhose on the neighbour's Persian rug and climbed onto the futon.

Day Two Thousand
Ashley bought into a Kapunda practice with his share from the narrow Queen St apartment.

Roberta bought a goldfish and moved in next door.

Andrew Craig

The Lepidopterist

The wings of a butterfly are a peculiarity of nature. Their beauty is paramount to anything created by mankind. Their fine delicacy and exquisitely complex patterning have created wonderment throughout history, being the inspiration for countless artworks. For a thousand generations we have watched these specks of colour flitter about us and have been carried away on their wings, away from our day-to-day lives, all the time without the slightest cognition of their most incredible facet:

The wings of most species of butterfly carry no pigment whatsoever. They are essentially colourless. Instead of having any inherent properties of colour, light is reflected, refracted, bent and twisted. As water vapour bends light into a rainbow, as a crystal separates colour from colour, so do the wings of the butterfly, but with more precision than a modern hologram.

As the dyes of the butterfly collector's shirt fade to white, his collection of specimens remains pristine and perfect. The complex three-dimensional, light-bending patterns of the wings are formed of a material more pure than fibre-optic cable. They exist only on a molecular scale. They can be seen only by an electron microscope. They are not understood and cannot be replicated.

We build atomic bombs, machine guns, tanks, cities, aeroplanes and spacecraft. We have learnt to inoculate ourselves against disease and reality. We have learnt to fly to the stars, to defy God's quarantine zone. But, at the end of the day, we are still just chasing that butterfly, and it keeps on flying through our net.

One day we will catch it. Technology will advance. It always does. The strongest, most intelligent hunter with his

spear once ran from the lion. The lion has since become the
sport-prey of the lazy businessman with his rifle. We all
know this. But, by the time we catch the butterfly, we will
already be dealing with its big brother ...

*   *   *

David was a hunter.

He looked out into the bustling marketplaces of Bangkok.
A crowd thronged about him, thrusting products in his face.

'Sixty baht.'

'Two-hundred baht.'

He pushed his way through them; he had something
more important in his sights than trinkets and snakes. He
could sense it was near, could feel a tickle at the back of his
throat.

In the age of stone, hunters fought against nature, their
evolutionary inadequacies overcome by primitive technologies. They were weaker, slower, less cunning and had senses
that left them practically deaf and blind when compared with
their prey. But Mother Nature had given them a gift, a mistake that would lead to the end of her rule, an administrative
oversight that threatened evolution itself: The opposing
thumb.

A child of the age of plastics, born of steel in the forges of
the Black Library, David continued the tradition of his
ancient counterparts.

He cleared his brain of conscious thought and let his
mind flow out onto the streets, searching for his prey,
sniffing for resonant traces.

To understand this ensuing conflict, we must imagine a
culture so advanced that it had broken apart the natural
order, it had defied nature and had developed its technologies
so far as to force us into an era of post-Darwinistic de-
evolution. A world in which the gene pool was devoid of
chlorine. In which the millions of bad genetic mutations
survived along-side the few good. Where the dumb, the
weak, the sickly survived alongside the strong. A world at war
with nature.

David travelled down the street, left, right, on and on. His eyes closed, he felt his way about the massed streets.

Now that we have broken with natural selection, now that we have reached escape velocity and burst into the unknown, we should be able to forget about nature. Ignore it and keep going. We have reached the peak of evolution; we have broken the chain. But there is no peak of evolution. Since the beginning of humanity we have believed that we lived at the end of history, unable to conceive of what may come after us. We have endlessly forgotten that evolution moves in a slow, inexorable cycle. We have forgotten that it was apathy that reigned in the centuries before the dinosaur's comet, in the decades before the end of the woolly mammoth's ice age, in the years before the white moth's black smog. And now, once again, apathy was ready to claim another victim.

David's vision focused on an old man bundled against the doorway of a shack. Everything faded into insignificance around him. There was nothing left but David and the old man, but the old man was no man at all.

You see, whilst the evolution of those technologically advanced nations stagnated, they forgot about those formless multitudes who lubricated the machinery of the industrial age. Those who required intelligence, willpower and strength merely to survive. In whose bodies a constant battle raged between health and disease. In whose bodies welled ancient strands of genetic code long ago forgotten …

They were known as post-terrestrials, neo-humans and freaks. But, generally, they were not known of at all.

That was where David came in.

He knew about them. He understood that his foes were the next step in evolution. He knew that nature had an uncanny ability to survive, to innovate. He knew that, at the end of the day, his battle was probably a futile one. His only hope was that the technology that coursed through his veins was enough to break the cycle of nature.

It was too late to turn back, humanity had come too far to give everything to its successor. We were in a one round no-holds-barred death-match with Mother Nature, and she had better be wearing her lucky shoes.

The old man stood. He and David stared at one another. The post-terrestrial versus Frankenstein's monster.

The old man's rags slivered away revealing his true form. He was the one who was many. He was the one that knew the farthest galaxies existed only in the deepest oceans. He was the one who knew that time and space were not curved about each other, but, instead, existed perpendicular. He was the one who twisted reality in on itself until it popped like a balloon. He was The One.

He breathed the vacuum of space and fed on life itself. To gaze into his eyes was to gaze upon the enormity of infinity itself, it was to understand everything, to understand our place in the universe and, consequently, to go insane. He was everything and nothing.

Static charges built up around the two as each waited for the other to make their move.

They simply watched and waited.

Lighting burst forth from the earth, and fire tore apart the heavens as the very fabric of space buckled and twisted with the weight of these two titans. Day became night as time itself imploded and split in two.

And they waited.

Those in the streets were melded into columns, buried alive and burst apart in the frozen wastes of space as they flickered out of reality, only to re-appear when the Earth had spun a thousand kilometres on its axis.

And still they waited.

The Earth tore itself apart beneath them, spurting forth lava and steam, exposing the fiery hells below.

And they waited.

Humanity was re-born three times, before re-emerging in its original form.

And they waited.

They would have waited for aeons, if space and time had not been torn apart from one another. They would have waited for …

There. A flinch. A moment of weakness. David tore the

universe in two, twisting the post-terrestrial out of existence.

Space-time rearranged itself into a new but stable form. Limited human minds persuaded themselves that this was the way it had always been and that the laws of physics were immutable.

David left for his next challenge.

* * *

Returning to the Black Library, David met with his masters.

'You have done excellently, David. We know that you have not been with us long, but your first job will also be your last. We are afraid our mission here, your mission here, is finished. There is only one question before you leave, David. Do you believe in a god?'

'I only believe in the mission.'

'Well, then. Maybe you should pick one.'

And, with a simple thought, the post-post-terrestrial tore David out of time and space so that he had never been and never would be. Reality was rearranged, his existence disappeared, and his story was unwritten, word by

* * *

And, once again, we are left chasing that butterfly, chasing it until the end ...

A Contemplation of a Camera

You do nothing but open and close,   and let things in, and out
like my mouth.   But you do not digest   I must do it for you.
                    You watch the world, blinkered.
Things go in,   **twisted**, *distorted*, <u>filtered</u>,   only a fraction recorded.
    You pretend that you see everything.
        You pretend you know everything.
        You pretend we can trust you.
            You pretend that you show everything.
                You pretend that this sky is white and that tree is black.
                You ignore the term 'dynamic range'.
                But it is my fault for not controlling you.
            It is my fault for trusting your single lens and your reflex.
        It is my fault for trusting your metered light.
        It is my fault for trusting your autofocus.
It is my fault for trusting you.
If only I could stamp 'Ricoh' on my frontal opening and
    deny culpability.
If only my deficiencies came without responsibilities.
If only I had more than one chance to get it right.
If only I could throw away my mistakes.
If only I could bracket my life,
        if only I could do it three times,
            once too much
            once too little
            once, just right.
If only I had automatic flash synchronisation.
        I don't know why.   I should throw you away,
                    Like a cheap disposable,
                        But I am just as fallible.
                    I see just as little.
                    I assume just as much.
    I can have no understanding   of those things to the left and right.
                of those things up and down.
                of those things too light.
                and too dark.

And, after all, we both use film.
I know you are shy.   You only open up to me for a sixtieth of a second.
        You may not be a Cannon,
                Or a Nikkon
                Or an Olympus
        But you are a Ricoh, and why not.
        They call you cheap knock off,
                but a rose by any other name …
We are more alike than you realise,   Do I not have a lens?
    I have two.
        I, too, automatically adjust my exposure due to weather conditions
        shorts for summer,
                pants for winter.
And if you push my buttons, do I not go into action?

So, why can't you love me? Why can't you see,
That my heart was made for you,
        And your cast alloy body for me.

The Chemical Dependency Shanty

A Sequence of Sonnets

The corp'rate man walks with his corp'rate gait,
Don't miss that meeting! Don't want to be late!
He's wond'ring why his nose is bleeding,
I'll tell you why, it's on cocaine he's been feeding.
Why did he snort that powder so white?
He needs the rush, he's been up all night
Making corp'rate deals with corp'rate friends,
Any means just, when for corp'rate ends,
For his corp'rate house, his corp'rate life,
His corp'rate child and corp'rate wife,
He corp'rately runs for his corp'rate meeting
And gives corp'rate people a corp'rate greeting.
His body is sweaty, his clothes are messed,
But the meeting is cancelled for a corp'rate blood test.

Oh Hippie, oh Hippie, you are so green,
I can but wonder where your pants have been
And when, by you, a bathtub was last seen.
Wearing druggie shirts and jacket of tan,
Oh Hippie, oh Hippie, you are the man
Who would drive a Volkswagen combi-van.
Your skin pallid white, your body is lean,
And you sport the moustache worn by a teen.
In saving the world you are awfully keen,
You refuse to flush whenever you can.
No matter how hot, you use not a fan,
You eat only bean curd fried in a pan.
With all of these troubles, how do you cope?
Can the answer be found in your room full of dope?

Who's that man, there upon the street,
Who wears no shoes upon his feet?
His sight is odd and does appal,
He lives at Saint Vincent de Paul.
His clothes are old and kind of smelly.
He has no food inside his belly.
He walks the streets, sings top-forty hits
And takes from the garbage your soiled bits.
He's in the gutter, he grumbles, he burps.
Needs your money to live, spends it on turps.
The winter cold, the body numb.
He is the archetypal Bum.
His clothes are muddy, their fitting is loose
And easily formed into a noose.

A Book of Genesis

On the first day

It was the pain that drove me here. Not physical pain. Not such a subordinate pain as that which plagues those around me, as they whinge and complain. Not such a meaningless pain, which drives them to aspirin and alcohol. I have never felt that pain since the accident. They say that my spinal cord was severed. I believe it was a case of pure and complete sensory overload. The noise of a thousand cymbals crashing. The feeling of a thousand shards of red-hot steel piercing my skin. The view of a thousand drops of blood. After that, my mind just gave up, determined never to feel another thing again.

On the second day

After just one night here, I must say that it is depressing to be surrounded by my own kind. I was told so often that it would be refreshing to talk to those going through the same thing I am. I suppose this would be true, if I were not surrounded by such morons. I cannot even escape, subjected as I am to the will of a grinning nurse, with thighs like jelly and a moustache more prominent than my own.

On the third day

As I sit in the garden, as helpless as always, I see something in the distance, under the shade of a eucalyptus tree. At first I believe it to be merely another session of physical therapy, but then I recognise the person in the wheelchair as Ms Mighall, whom I met with the day before and whom had been introduced to me as a paraplegic of ten years. She stands. I am sure she stands. On her own. Without help, without levers or pulleys, smoke or mirrors, she stands. I know they are doing advanced research here, but I never dreamed I would see such a thing. I am still unsure that I have.

On the fourth day

They said it was a breakthrough. It was a breakthrough all right; I could hear them breaking right through my skull. They said that although I would be conscious, I would feel no pain. When will they understand that consciousness is a state of pain? If hearing the perpetual whining and my vision shaking as the drill enters my skull is not painful, then what is? When will they understand that pain is a mental state, not a physical one? When will they understand that I would give anything to feel again, even if it was the feeling of them tinkering with my mind like children with a new toy?

On the fifth day

Today I stand for the first time. Only for a brief moment before my atrophied muscles give way, but everything looks different from a few feet higher. I just have to push a button and up I go. The rest of the day is spent isolating muscle groups, anaesthetising them and then trying to stand again, in the hope of achieving a better, more balanced posture. They say the text books are wrong, that everyone is different. They say it will be months of fine-tuning and muscle development before the computer learns to make me stand, not to mention walk. It will take a little longer to learn to do it directly, without anyone pushing buttons. I never could have believed that all of this would happen so fast, even after I realised what they were doing here. I thought I would be in bed for a week before I even regained consciousness, they say the operation was actually very simple. Just a pinprick hole. It did not sound like they were making a pinprick hole. They also say the tremors I have been having are normal, just the body and computer learning to communicate with each other.

On the sixth day

A wave of strange sensations floods my mind as they insert the diskette and push go, allowing direct contact between my body and mind. It will be weeks before my brain begins to understand the input and match it to my distant memory. The fat nurse kisses me on the lips and I see a rainbow of colours. I shall have to tell them about that.

On the seventh day

I have already begun to distinguish touch on the various parts of my body. To distinguish pleasure from pain. Today they have to make adjustments to my implant. They say they cannot be done with the remote unit and must be done manually. They say it may be a little uncomfortable, but they would not be touching anything living and there was no reason for me to be unconscious. Laying me on my front, they use a drill to remove the screws on the back of my neck. I try to shut out the noise. It reminds me of what they did six days ago. It reminds me of the crunch of bone overcome by the machine. It reminds me of what happened fifteen years ago. It reminds me of what happened to my wife and daughter. It reminds me of not being able to wipe the tears from my eyes. I try to shut out the noise and think of the footprints I will leave in the snow once this is over. Suddenly the tremors begin again. I feel my arm beginning to shake. I feel my teeth clenching tighter and tighter. I hear the technicians begin to panic. I feel my body convulsing. I hear them run for help. I feel my teeth pop like firecrackers, one by one. I feel saliva and blood drip down my face. I feel my head slam up and down on the bed. I feel the drill bit entering the back of my head.

I do not feel a thing.

Little Wonder

An apple perches precariously on the peak of the table.
Golden delicious.
Two dollars forty-nine a kilo.
I wonder what lies beneath that golden sheath,
Hidden within its dappled skin?
An ancient temptation that led to original sin.
What works of art were inspired by these sweet treats?
One of Shakespeare's shows, one of Keats's feats?
What drives us to crush
Its flesh into mush?
To sprinkle it with spices drawn from across the land,
To bind it with cinnamon,
To confine it in muffins?
What secret does it hold?
What mystical marvels?
What celestial delight?
Does it help us write essays?
Does it help us to fight?
Does it make us a profit?
Help us see in the night?
Can I, with it, fly,
And shine forth bright light?
Does it remove me from disease,
Does it remove me from plight?
There must be more!
Something kept of sight,
More than just something for vegans to feed on,
More than just fruit for children to loot.

No,
It's just an apple.

Rebecca Coles

In our Universe, Stars Aglow

In our universe, stars aglow;
Astral angels of beaming light.
Magical wonder they bestow.

At dusk heaven opens their window
And night they appear in our sight.
In our universe, stars aglow;

Planets mysteriously grow
While a stellar shoots through the night.
Magical wonder they bestow,

Showering rays on us below
To share their enigmatic light.
In our universe, stars aglow.

Their deep secrets I want to know,
Instead they nest silently bright.
Magical wonder they bestow.

I yearn not to hear the cock crow,
Alas nature ignores my plight.
In our universe, stars aglow.
Magical wonder they bestow.

Still there tomorrow

A bridge leads the way across
To the other side of loss.
Where journeys meet,
Anger retreats
And love abounds among us.
Friendships are made only to
Be tested by change, though true
Friends remain rich.
But will the bridge
Still be there tomorrow?
Giving shelter from the rain
Sweethearts gather, hearts beating.
Light from the sun
Streams on them. Fun
Childhood memories of past;
Underneath where shadows are cast,
Collecting the tadpoles there.
They grow up fast
But the bridge outlasts,
Still there tomorrow.
Hellos, goodbyes, sorrow
And happiness. Something lost,
Something found. I feel
The bridge will still
Be there tomorrow. Tortured
Soul hiding within a scorched
Heart. Springboard for suicide.
For her there are
Distances to cross, far
Beyond the earthy plane, to
Find peace within herself anew.
Though she is gone and life is
Changed, the bridge'll
Still be there tomorrow.

What's in the Magazines?

What will I read today, now let me see?
Who is in vogue and most of all what's hot?
Wonder is she's had a facelift or not?

Miracle diet, strict exercise plans,
How could I get by without those food bans
Or the wise question: are you too fat? Must

Get help from the mag's specialist guide.
A facelift, tummy-tuck and lipo is all
You need to look like a supermodel.

Photo specials: stars share their secrets. 'I
Don't have a life outside a mag.' Fashion
Is for me and experiencing passion

Thanks to Reader's Fiction. And when I have
A problem the columnist'll tell me how
To solve it. I will do the questionnaire now.

It asks questions and I give answers with
My views. Like I have time when I work a
Twenty-four hour day, but it's okay

I can't complain – no one will listen. So
I'll read my Star Guide – it will see me through,
Can call 1902's Astro guru.

I went through with the surgery advised,
I'm so pleased with my new face and body
I look like Barbie, you know, the Dolly.

I just can't eat or go out in the sun
As I could risk losing my perfection.
I'll simply stay inside and read the gossip section

And I'll take 5 out of a woman's day
To spot the flaws of stars. That's bazaar. New wife?
Eighth time? How things change. I suppose that's life!
And the magazines are always right.

Natasha Alexander

Ode to a Friend

To some, he must appear a clown,
Unusually tall and especially slim,
He walks this earth in happy pants
And a smile seems forever stuck to my face.

I would say he is my best friend
And they can be hard to find.
You know, someone that requires no effort,
Just a look of warmth and a smile.

So uncanny is his ability
To makes a bad day good.
And by casting a smile in my direction
My problems just melt away.

His shinning eyes are but a window
So we can glance inside.
Within his presence I feel happiness,
I hope he never goes away.

He asks for nothing, but gives the world,
People seem forever to need his service.
How could one person be so selfless?
You do a good job, my friend.

He sees in people their goodness,
And looks beyond what society see.
He is a friend to everyone,
And most especially one to me.

Book of Life

Life is merely a novel,
Though an adventurous one.
Full of discoveries and love,
Yet heart ache and pain.
But, as each chapter ends,
A hand will reach out to
Turn the page
And reveal a new one.

And you will charge head first
Through many a chapter,
Leaving behind characters
But meeting many new ones.
And it will remain so
Until the end is near.

With the turn of this last page
I want to see a being,
Carved beautifully
By none more artistic
Than Time herself.
Then, as the book is closed forever,
I pray to Time to leave alone
The smile she chiselled on your face.

Ↄ

Thirsty for the rain,
The dry ground encourages her.
She lets her tears fall.

ↄ

Sally Engelhardt

A Greener Existence

S he knew its eyes were fixed on her, even though she could not see it. The snake had found its way under the bed and there it stayed.

She'd gone out the back door for a cigarette and turned her back for a minute. The late afternoon was too beautiful to miss. She'd only been there before when she was very little but she was reminded of the aura of the place as she watched the sun drip from the horizon, the sky painted pink and orange by light cloudy brush-strokes. When she returned to the door of her room she saw the last of the snake's tail disappear over the threshold.

Now, sitting on the wide dresser, her back pressed against the mirror, she watched the place where she last saw the snake. Of all things to be terrified of, snakes were the worst, and now, of all times, she had to be confronted by one. Everything else she had control of, but nature was about to beat her – if she let it. Jumping up on the dresser had knocked her belongings out of the way. Designer-labelled perfume bottles lay with a mixed assortment of quality conditioners and the newest shades that could only be bought by appointment.

Trust Arnie to pick the most remote place on earth. After not seeing this country for a good decade, its harshness surprised her, unwrapping her from the cotton wool existence she lavished upon herself. Arnie thought it best, though, if she was a long way away. If the deal went bad she'd have time on her hands. That's what he'd said anyway.

Arnie was easily placated, which was exactly what she'd wanted. She'd told him that 'the dust would hurt her eyes and the sun might fade her hair.'

'Don't be ridiculous,' he growled. 'You'll only be there for a day. You've got enough crap in that bag to protect you from nuclear war.' She'd batted her eyelids meekly and agreed with him.

She thought she saw something move. Bracing herself against the mirror, she felt down to the drawers. Keeping her eyes locked on the snake, she opened the top drawer and felt for her gun. Its silvery texture touched her fingers. She fumbled the heavy weapon into her grip. She yanked it out of the drawer. Pointing it at the snake, she mumbled, 'You're not fucking this plan up.' She could see movement under the bed. She wanted its head. 'Come on,' she urged. There was a slow flick of the tail. And then the head. *BOOM!* The gun exploded. The snake was a writhing nerve. The metallic smell of gunshot pervaded the cool, dusky air.

*   *   *

She had been walking along Regent Street for almost four minutes. Entering the marbled foyer she smoothed out her skirt. She'd had her suit made the week before. She wanted something convincing and she hadn't spared a cent in getting it. The taupe suede hugged her every curve but was conservative in length. One didn't want to attract more attention than was necessary – the manager was all she was aiming for. The tailored leather briefcase rested in her cool fingers. Its weight evenly distributed by the expert cut. The sum of her worries she had control of. Timing every breath kept her forehead from sparkling and her hands from clamming up. She looked good, she had the documents, she even had Diana call them to let them know the exact amount. One final adjustment of the scarf and a smooth of the hair. She strode into the bank at exactly one forty-five.

Clack … Clack … Clack … She could feel people's eyes on her as she listened to the sound of her footfalls, amplified by the walls of polished rock. She looked only straight ahead, her eyes searching for the suit she was assured would appear. A balding man came from behind the staffed counter. She nodded her head towards him as he uttered her name.

'Tom Grier's office is this way ma'am.'

'Thank you,' she replied. She was led toward the rear of the main room. A door was ajar and the balding man gestured she enter.

She could turn back now and she would be safe. She would finish the deal with Arnie and get out clean. She would continue to do these jobs that she detested and would be Arnie's 'Little Woman' until wrinkles appeared on her face, reminding Arnie that he needed a newer model. She was not afraid of Arnie, nor was she afraid of the people she crossed. But to think she would be doing this job until *they* didn't want her anymore repulsed her. She proceeded through the door; there was no turning back. The next two days would pass and she would be invisible. No more Arnie. No more deals. She could hear her name being called.

She flashed an ivory smile to the man in front of her with his hand outstretched.

Enthusiastically he shook her hand, 'Finally, you and I meet,' he grinned.

'Yes,' she replied demurely. His name matched the etching on the door, though his face was not what she imagined.

The briefcase was carefully placed beside her as she sat in a luxurious chair, its comfort fuelling her resolve.

'Its been a lovely day, hasn't it?' Tom asked her.

'I hear it will be improving.'

'Now if you could read and sign this form. Your associate, Diana, rang this morning to confirm the exact figure. Five million, US?'

'That's correct,' she spoke with a lowered voice for a more professional sound. She read the details of her deposit and held the handcrafted pen in her relaxed fingers.

'If I could take a look at the title deeds, then we will be on our way,' Tom looked at her.

She placed the case on the table and opened it, revealing the documents. Handing them to Tom, she could feel her foot start to bounce nervously. She stopped it immediately, opting to cross her ankles under the chair.

'Would you like some tea while you wait?'

'That would be fine, thank you,' she smiled at Tom.

'May I?' he gestured toward the briefcase still on the table.

'Certainly.'

He paused before leaving, as if to say something. She averted her gaze and he left the office. Shortly after, a steaming cup of tea was offered to her by the same balding man she had met earlier.

She thought about the origin of the tea. Who picked it and at what time of year. She didn't allow herself to think about Arnie, who wasn't meant to call but could at any minute to check up on her. She didn't think about Tom Grier seeing through her guise and calling the CIB. She thought, instead, of the people in China who picked tea leaves, one by one, rain or shine. They picked the leaves because they had no choice.

An enormous sense of triumph had her heart racing and footsteps falling in quick succession as she strode down the steps of the bank. 'Diana, please,' was directed into her mobile phone as she scanned the street for a taxi. 'It's all done ... Absolutely ... He did ... I'm about ten minutes away.'

The taxi sped through the afternoon traffic and she arrived outside the café she and Diana always patronised. Adjusting her scarf over her hair and slipping her sunglasses up the bridge of her nose, she thanked the taxi driver. She spotted Diana already at a table.

'Helena, darling, how *are* you?' Diana kissed her on the cheek.

Rolling her eyes at Diana's exuberance she replied, 'I'm just glad to be out of there. I kept expecting to be questioned about it but he was happy with all the paperwork.'

'I told you the suit would do it, we must remember that we are only dealing with men,' Diana said knowingly.

Helena smiled at her as the waiter placed their coffee on the table.

*   *   *

There was a loud clunk against the door. Then there was some deep throated cursing followed by scratching of keys against the door. Finally Arnie managed to enter the room, he was puffing and his forehead was glistening. 'I don't know why they have lifts when it's quicker to walk!' was his greeting.

'Oh, Arnie, its good to see you at last. I thought you had been caught,' came the giggling reply. 'Would you like a drink?'

'Don't have time for messing around. Just a shot will be fine.'

Helena poured scotch into the glass and gave it to him.

'Right, let's go. Hurry up,' he growled. 'I've got a car waiting.'

' Okay, Arnie. Keep your hair on,' she replied softly.

He glared at her as she collected her bag.

In the lift Arnie looked her in the eye, 'Quickly and quietly, no shopping, just straight to the car and go. Got it?'

She nodded.

They walked through the foyer together. She had put her baseball cap on and glasses. She didn't want anyone spotting her black and white image on a camera. Arnie couldn't have cared less, of course, but that was the way he worked. And she dare not let him know why she was different.

Arnie grabbed her arm to steer her toward the car he had hired. He was never one to miss a chance at drawing attention to himself.

Helena looked at him with raised eyebrows, 'My hair might get messed up.'

'Just get in. I'll see you tomorrow.'

She put her bag on the backseat and watched Arnie put the briefcase in the boot. She opened the half door and sank into the lush leather seat. 'Red's my colour too,' she gushed to Arnie who was waiting for her to leave.

She revved the engine and was soon driving along Highway One, the morning sun thrilling her with its warmth.

* * *

The snake took some time to cease writing and the mess had taken a couple of hours to clean up. Helena looked at herself in the mirror while warm water rushed over her fingers. Her phone demanded her attention with its shrill ring. Knowing it would be Arnie, she took her time drying her hands before answering.

'Where have you been?' Arnie snarled.

'Oh, Arnie, I was polishing my nails and I didn't want to smudge them by doing anything in a hurry.'

'Whatever.'

'Are you checking up on me? I nearly got lost when I ran out of suburbs on the map,' she giggled for effect. 'But I got here fine, the car was really nice to dr…'

'Listen, this is what we're doing tomorrow. You'll meet me at the Castle Hotel, we'll swap cars and then you're going to the airport.'

'The airport?' Helena sounded worried. 'Arnie, what are you doing?' Concern gripped her. 'This wasn't the plan. Did you lose today? They said that it was all fixed. Are they going to get you?'

'You don't have anything to worry about. Let me worry about the details.'

'You know I don't like these changes … ' She turned on the tears. 'What if I forget where I'm going. I might not find this place. You know I like to check things out before we do business. What if they know I'm there? I don't want to let you down,' she sobbed into the phone.

'For god's sake, stop crying. I'll message you the address, you'll look it up on your map and then you'll be there tomorrow at three. Got it? You'll be fine.' The phone went dead.

'Shit, shit, *shit!*' she exclaimed as she punched at the phone numbers. 'Di, darls, there's been an amendment.' Helena said tersely.

'No worries, love. Will the show be starting earlier tomorrow?' It was hard to fluster Diana.

'You could say that. My appointment just got moved to three.'

'I'll set everything up for three then.'

'Is that feasible?'

'Don't worry, I'll speak to Tabatha, they owe me a favour anyway.'

'Cheers,' Helena hung up.

The early morning chill was leaving the air as Helena placed her bags in the car. She looked toward the sun that was beginning to illuminate the landscape. *Today will go smoothly*, she told herself. *Everything is in place; it will all run smoothly*. She looked at the beautifully crafted briefcase. It was nothing like the type Arnie used. Hers was sophisticated and stylish, made from the same piece of leather so the colour was uniform. She placed it next to the briefcase Arnie had given her. The contents of each case were carefully laid to avoid disturbance during transit. Each was terrifying in its own right. She placed Arnie's case in the boot, while hers sat on the back seat directly behind her. Her bag of clothes and her beauty case sat alongside it.

She lit a cigarette and took a long drag. Surveying the country that she had once loved, she felt a pang at the price she had paid. She admired its beauty as she took in the vista before her. A flock of galahs were warming up to a noisy din in a tree behind her. They took flight and their wings whooshed above her head as they headed into the sunrise. This was Helena's cue to leave. The thrill of power surged through her as she spun the wheels, leaving a dusty curtain behind her.

Several hours later she pulled into the driveway of the apartment block Diana had rented for the week. She grabbed her bags and briefcase and ran upstairs. Opening the door, Diana looked at her with raised eyebrows. 'Nice hair.'

Helena looked in a nearby mirror and they laughed. They looked at each other and amusement soon gave way to serious looks.

'When am I due at the bank?' Helena asked.

'One forty-five. I'll drop you around the corner; you'll walk from there. Catch a cab back to Brassy's. We'll be there until two forty-five. I'll have the car. Then we'll go.'

Helena headed to the bathroom as Diana gave her instructions.

'Your suit got here yesterday, nice job.' Diana shouted over the sound of the shower.

'I know, it's a shame we can't take Madge with us.'

'She'd die if she knew what it was for.' Diana laughed and looked at her watch.

* * *

Helena practised her breathing while she drove down Liverpool Street. The open top of Arnie's car allowed the wind to rush around her. She tightened the scarf around her head, adjusting her earpiece inside its camouflage. Turning left onto Brady Terrace she checked in one last time. 'Dan, I'm completing the last leg. Can you hear me OK?'

'Loud and clear, Lane, see you soon.'

She could see the Castle Hotel getting closer. Her heart was pounding in her chest, but her breathing was calm, as always. She slowed and pulled into the car park. Driving very slowly, she finally saw Arnie.

'I've found the Apple, there'll be changeover soon,' Helena spoke quietly.

Arnie nodded his head in her direction. Helena flashed him a big smile. Just as she did she noticed flashing lights on the road. She was pulling into the space next to Arnie's when she saw the police entering the car park. She looked at Arnie in horror. He looked equally shocked. He swung around the car and got in the passenger seat next to her.

'Don't do anything just yet. Get out some lipstick or something. Make it look like I'm waiting for you. Why are they here? Who did you tell?' he growled fiercely.

'Don't make me cry, Arnie, my mascara will run,' she said as she adjusted the mirror to look in. She could see the police still had their lights flashing but were not coming near them.

'They aren't coming over here. Maybe they don't know who we are?'

'Look, you take the other car, I'll take this one. Get out. Go!'

Helena carefully got out of the convertible and into the sedan that Arnie had driven.

Arnie got out to swap sides, 'Is the case in the boot?' he growled, nodding toward the rear of the car.

'Of course, Arnie. Are they coming this way yet?' Helena's shaky voice made Arnie swing around to look.

'No. Get on the road. I'll call you with a place to meet. Go!' he roared at her.

Helena wound up the window. Composure gained, she reversed out of the parking space.

On the road, she checked in with Diana. 'I'm heading north on Brady, where are you?'

'Corner of Lincoln and First. Turn left down Webb, then second right.'

Turning, she accelerated. Helena sped down the side street and turned again. 'I'm on First, where are you?'

'We're quite a way down. You should be here soon.'

'I am, I can see you, great.' Helena sighed. She pulled left. The car halted. Helena leapt out and ran across to Diana's waiting car. A woman dressed the same as Helena with a scarf on her head crossed the road and got into the empty vehicle.

The car lurched as Diana accelerated. They went over the main road and headed south for the airport.

'What time do we go?'

'Four to Sydney and we head out from there.'

Helena's phone chirped loudly.

'Arnie?' she called.

'Right I'm heading to …'

'Arnie, one of them is following me, I don't know what to do … ' Helena let her voice break.

'Jesus,' came Arnie's gruff reply

'He's not very close but I went down a side street and he kept following me,' Helena sobbed.

'Jesus Christ. Take the car back then, there's nothing in it. It's from Budget at the airport. Get a cab from there. Meet me at my place. They can't arrest you for doing that.'

' Okay,' was the teary reply.

'Jen, it goes to Budget at the airport. Then you can disappear,' Diana spoke into her mic.

'What's with the cops?' Helena asked incredulously as she removed her earpiece and microphone.

'I put some cream on your pie,' Diana gave her a sly look. 'Remember Little Tim?'

'Yeah.'

'Well, he's back in town. He took me out to dinner when you were gone and I asked him to do me a favour.'

'You are … ' Helena trailed off.

'Well, it gave Uncle Arnie something to think about so it couldn't turn nasty.'

'Thanks,' Helena said sarcastically.

* * *

Helena gazed out the window past Diana. The Pacific Ocean was a deep darkness beneath them and the lights of Sydney were almost out of sight. She looked over the aisle, through the window on the other side of the airplane. Not seeing anything, she sighed.

Sipping her tea, Diana looked at Helena with a smirk. 'I wonder how Arnie's going?'

'Who cares?' Helena said seriously. 'Anyway, I gave him something to think about.'

'What are you talking about,' Diana raised her eyebrows.

'Well, you know that snake I shot?'

A Little Country Town

We pulled off the road, onto the footpath, or what would have been if there was anything to distinguish it from the road. There was the *Age* sign out the front of a building. We assumed they sold the state's paper. This place couldn't be too out of the way if they had the paper. 'General Store' announced a sign above the door. And general it was – a bit of everything, not much of anything. Plenty of newspapers, though. I wandered down the aisle, seeing if I could use anything from this general store. I whistled as I walked, hoping to attract someone's attention. Glancing over to the counter I saw no-one.

I walked up to the counter, putting the paper down, 'Hello?' I enquired.

'Coming, coming,' a bustling, matronly woman came from out the back somewhere with a big grin on her face. 'Sorry, just popped out for a moment. Is that all, the paper? We've got a special on bread, being Sunday and all, a dollar a loaf, love, but it's frozen – doesn't keep well otherwise. Whaddya say?' She grinned at me some more. For a woman who didn't speak to many people in a day, she sure was making up for it now.

'Ahh, no, just the paper … Oh, and a Mars.'

'They're good, aren't they? That'll be two-eighty thanks, love, nice day today, just passing through, eh? Lots of people do – no one ever stays though! Not much to see here, sorry,' she giggled, as if it was her fault the town was in the middle of nowhere. 'Twenty change for you, love, can't keep chatting all day,' she grinned again, 'Bye!' And she bustled off.

Trusting soul.

Tucking the paper under my arm, I crossed the road with Ann, my driving partner. I didn't have to look for cars but out of habit I did. I eyed a park bench some way off in a reserve. When I got to it I checked to see if it was dry. The lichen made a soft covering on the hard wooden seat. We sat down gingerly, anticipating what, I wasn't sure. Relieved, I peered through the orange foliage to see the white clouds floating through the atmosphere.

Something caught the corner of my eye. Jogging through the reserve was a pointer-type dog. Nose to the fragrant carpet weaving his way slowly towards us. He came quite close, still with his nose to the ground, ignoring us.

'Hey!' I called.

The dog scuttled sideways, glaring, 'Woof!' A pause. And then he was away again. Ann and I looked at each other and giggled. I looked for an owner or companion. Finding none, I wondered if anyone lived nearby.

Ann poured coffee from a thermos she brought. The familiar aroma seemed out of place among the musty, earthy smells of the park. I could see a swing set to my right. One of the seats was missing and the chains were very rusty. The only indication of a play area was the swing frame itself, any sand underneath had been covered by many seasons of leaf fall.

Looking left, I could see an old cottage some way off, making up half the number of houses on this side of the street. The vines and bushes had taken over the nearest side wall. There was only darkness to be seen through the broken windows. One solitary pillar held up the sagging verandah. An ancient armchair furnished the front porch.

There was another house further down. Its garden wasn't as shabby as the cottage but its dishevelled appearance revealed that its inhabitants had deserted the place some time ago. Looking behind me, the General Store seemed more life-like. The adjoining house and garden hadn't seen a lawnmower in a while, but there was a well worn path from the door to the front gate. The few houses next to it were much the same. The church a little way to the left of the General Store had a recent service date and the garden was bare, except for the roses that had been recently pruned and mulched. Quite a few headstones, some not old at all, could be seen through the rose garden.

I heard a rumbling from a distance. I turned my head left and right to determine where it was coming from. Right, it was coming from the east. Rumble, rumble, the noise got louder and louder. The semi-trailer could be clearly heard owing to the absence of features on the landscape. The exhaust brakes resounded through the air as the semi hit the 60 km zone. The buildings seemed to hold their breath in anticipation. Roaring past us, the vehicle gained speed as it headed for the town's limit. The buildings sighed with relief. So did I.

'Wibbel Flat rush hour,' Ann said from behind me. 'Let's get out of here.'

Christa Mano

Coptotermes
(A variety of termite)

Endless drumming
Never ending humming
The noise infuriates me.

Infinite munching
Ceaseless marching
The source eludes me.

Immeasurable in number
Inexhaustible in hunger
Their presence haunts me.

My home perpetually warm
Multitudinous swarm
Their existence ignites me.

Numberless quantity
Perpetual ferocity
Their blindness enrages me.

Bereft of reason
In every season
Their hunger inflames me.

Battle lines drawn
I'll defeat the swarm
Their deaths will restore me.

Modernity

It all lies in the pages of paper leaves;
Fix your gardens, plant trees, paint your eaves.
Take heart, no land is beyond repair,
Follow all the instructions, with never a care.

When the gardens are done and all is abloom,
Surely it's time to redecorate your room.
Take heart, it can all be done in a trice,
And it can be fun, if you disregard price.

The garden is done, the house is delightful,
But look at yourself, your face is frightful.
Take heart, nevertheless, for all can be saved,
The surgeon will fix you, your face can be paved.

The magazines abound, our duty is clear,
To all their instructions we must adhere.
Plant, prune, pave; paint and redecorate,
All the pages will tell you it's never too late.

&

Bright green earthy mat
decorated nest of leaves:
the rat is hiding.

&

Simone Wise

The Sports Lesson

The oval is a sea of green. Too much green. An awful, sickly plastic green. The sun pierces down and I can feel it wrapping its heat around the back of my legs. *It's too hot for sport today. Can't we just go back inside and do work? Please God, make him force us to do lines or copy out the whole textbook. Please, please, please don't make me do this.*

Someone passes me the bottle of sun block, already slippery from greasy hands. I squeeze out too much, the slithering cool liquid drips out of my hand. I rub it into my legs. At first it looks like they're coated with a wash of white paint, then the original pink scrawny legs re-emerge. Its artificial smell is everywhere and it leaves my hands feeling like they've been rubbed in animal fat.

With limp, languid movements I follow the others to the middle of the oval. They're all laughing and gossiping like parakeets in a fruit tree. Girls flirt with boys, and boys squeeze them at the waist, or steal their hats. The girls shriek back in a pathetic attempt to look annoyed. There's something about wearing these shorts, with this chest-clinging polo shirt in such sultry weather. Those particular girls move more fluidly; their walk is the smooth sliding of waves onto the sand. Of course the boys notice this. Their voices become deeper and they stride with their heads higher. My head is lowered; I'm studying my sneakers as they trudge along the ground. They make a squeaking sound as they are pulled over the grass.

A booming voice reverberates in my ear, telling us slackers to hurry up or we'll have to run laps. *You're not in the army anymore Mr Hoffman, you don't have to bellow at us like we're soldiers.* Every time he starts a sentence, he emphasises the first word so much that it jolts me.

I can see it in all its morbid glory now. Surrounded by its blue mat disciples, the vault stands majestically on its wooden legs, sneering at me, daring me to even try to get over it. *I want to die. I want to develop a rare disease, preferably starting right now, so that I'll faint. Then I won't have to fail again; landing with a hollow thud, legs tingling from the shock and face burning with shame from their looks of contempt.*

We stand in a line as the man – standing so erect – yells out the next name on the list with a military sharpness. Each person takes a turn and I move closer and closer, step-by-step, to the front of the line. Fear grabs me by the back of the neck, pulling at the small hairs. My heart has grown so big with terror that it pushes against my chest, pressing into my lungs and rising up to my throat, clenching it tight. My eyes prick and burn as I take another step closer. As names are called out the alphabet moves further along and I realise with a churning, sinking feeling how close I am; how soon it's going to happen.

I don't want to do this. I can't. I can't do it. I can't. I've tried before and I couldn't, so I won't be able to this time. Please, please don't make me do it, you don't understand, I CAN'T. Why am I so hopeless? You're such an idiot. Everyone knows you won't be able to. They'll smirk when it's your turn to go up.

I clench my fists so tight that my fingernails leave red crescent shapes on my palms, a row of frowns. The person before me takes their turn. Jogging up, they take a single leap onto the trampoline and glide over, landing at the other side with a satisfied curtsy. Such sportsmanship. What a hero, making it look like it's the easiest thing in the world. *It probably is, it's just that you're so bloody hopeless you can't.* I feel so heavy, like my whole body is made of lead. I close my eyes and try to relax, seeing a haze of orange and yellow through my eyelids. My name is called and my eyes snap open. Silence. People look up from their chattering and all heads turn to me. I begin to run, eyes fixed on the figure ahead.

I can't do this. I really can't do this.

Laura Bombardieri

Grandma's house

Even before she entered the house, Anthia could smell that old familiar smell. It seemed to find a way of seeping through the walls and blending with the air outside. A mixture of old books and toast, fabric softener and dog. But was it an unpleasant smell? No. More of a distinct and powerful smell. One that was hard not to remember. A smell that seemed to remain, no matter how much Glen 20 was sprayed. Anthia even felt a fondness towards this smell, as it had been a part of her life for as long as she could remember. The smell belonged to her Grandmother's home; a place that she knew was special.

Anthia felt around in her pocket for the key, it lay there cold and lifeless in her hand. The old-fashioned style key flipped around in the keyhole; Anthia remembered it was a tricky lock. Inside, she drew the stiff pale curtains across to let in the warm afternoon sun. She looked around the room and noticed that some of the furniture was missing. It seemed so empty without all of Grandma's things. The room felt smaller, or was it bigger? Anthia wasn't certain but she was certain of one thing, it felt wrong.

She walked across the plush off-white carpet, lightly dragging her fingers along the polished oak piano along the way, as if trying to savour what was left. The kitchen felt cold. Anthia knew that this was the room in which Grandma spent most of her time. The warmness it used to hold was gone now and the kitchen felt naked. Anthia scanned the table, looking for the papers her mother had asked her to pick up. Next to the toaster was a yellow ceramic mug. Grandma's mug. Anthia stared into it. It was half filled with a cold brown liquid. Tea. Grandma drank a lot of tea. *How can it be … How can it be that Grandma was here drinking this tea just two days ago and now … now she is not here to finish it.* Tears burned her eyes and stung the inside of her nose. She wondered if there were any cells in that mug from Grandma and how could a part of her be living when she was dead. She looked away from the mug and sobbed loudly. Grandma's house was different now.

Rosella

While crossing the road,
I saw a Rosella bird sitting between the branches of a lush
    hedge.
Its feathers were an electrifying green,
The feathers around its head, a vibrant blue.
How beautiful, I thought.
As I completed the crossing of the road
And was much closer to this magnificent creature,
I saw that
It was just
An empty Sprite bottle someone had lodged in the
    bushes.

Gary Campbell

Magnolias

The town of Wanganui sits by the sluggish river of the same name. It is neither on a high plain or in a valley, but somewhere in between. The sun does not shine too much there. Neither does the wind and rain chill too keenly. At the river mouth grey seas pound cliffs and pill boxes left over from the Second World War. The land is always green, and insufferably so. The birds are small and brown and sing painfully pleasant songs.

In the middle of the town is Gonville Hill. One can see all of Wanganui from the top of the hill, but those who live on it rarely care to look. The sun can be beautifully warm up there, but the inhabitants seldom stand beneath it.

The hill is made of grey sand and supports nothing but hardy and un-exotic vegetation. There is a red brick church on it, set in an asphalt court where the parishioners complain about the sermon after mass and slander each other. When visitors enter the church they are struck by a notice in the porch that reads, in big black letters, WE NEED A WALL. The priest, Father Leonard, is very security conscious and constantly urged contributions for a wall to protect Gonville Hill. Eventually he got enough money and built the thing. But the notice didn't come down.

So Father Leonard and the other priests pass to and fro, treading their hill of sand, content in the thought that if their wall should fail them, the notice would not.

* * *

My name is Andrew. I was an outsider to Gonville, even while I was married to Susan who was born in the parish. She had gone when we started to build the wall.

I met her on a holiday. We liked each other. We were

both Roman Catholics. So it seemed a good idea to get married.

As I say, I was an outsider. I was an outsider to Susan and her world. I was an outsider to myself. We separated but Susan could not bring herself to sign the divorce papers and left town without a word. I could not leave Wanganui. I did not know myself there, but I did know something there. I knew that God lived in the church, in a little box with a red light over it. I knew that heaven was above and hell was below. And I knew that the priests told me what my place was between these two eternal chasms.

I did not cry for joy ever with Susan, but I did with Angela. Because of her I love to cry and I love to laugh. And I love to dance. I met her while I was working with some of the other parish men on the foundations of the wall.

'Hi, good lookin',' she said.

I was bare armed, shovelling dirt. I liked to show my arms off, but I would not have known what to do if a woman said something flirty. I smiled and said 'Hello.'

Angela was blonde with a round, tanned face. She wore jeans and a red sleeveless top. In her hair she wore a pink hibiscus. She spoke in a sort of song but without any hint of affectation.

I offered my hand from the bottom of the pit I had dug. 'I'm Andrew.'

'Yes, I know. All the parish ladies know about you.' She looked whimsically at my open palm, which was dirty and sweaty. 'I'm Angela, the school dance instructor. See ya later, gorgeous.' I blushed and smiled. I hoped I would see her again.

A few weeks later, on a Saturday morning, I was on the school oval teaching some of the schoolboys Australian Rules. I had just taken a pass and they cried, 'Let's tackle 'im!' So ten junior high school lads brought me down like jackals might bring down their prey. They laughed and shouted in their triumph.

'Boys! Boys! Get off him. Leave some for others.' It was Angela, laughing.

They got up. I threw them the ball and they began to play by themselves.

'The kids like you,' said Angela.

'I like them,' I said.

'You must be a good father.'

'My wife and I didn't get a chance to have kids. Would've liked to.'

'I'm sure you'll have your chance. It would be a crime against childhood if you didn't.'

I laughed. 'You hardly know me. How can you say things like that?'

'I can tell,' she replied.

'How's the dancing going?' I asked.

'Oh, so-so. The kids are enjoying the Waltz and the Foxtrot. Well, the girls are. But I want to encourage the children to have a sense of rhythm, to move with the music, not to obey it. You know what I mean?'

'No I don't.'

'Dance isn't something outside of us. It's something *inside* us. It's our being, our ego. It's the I that every human being wants to express. The way we dance expresses who we are. It frees us from inhibitions and barriers and lets us live.

'Now all these formal dances like waltz and tango are all very beautiful. I teach them. But in a sense they keep the individual locked up. We have to follow the steps. We become slaves to our feet, not the other way around. So I'd like to teach the kids to move with the music first. The way they want. I seem to be having trouble persuading Father Leonard to the same view.'

I was both fascinated and uneased by what she said. After I sent the boys home we walked and talked for a bit. Angela told me that she was a wanderer. She was happy enough to stay in a place, but not for long. For that reason she had never had a lasting relationship.

'I guess I just fly too fast and too high for most men,' she said. I could hear more than a sigh when she said that.

As I walked beside her, following the freshly marked white lines of the oval, I thought of what it would be like to be a wanderer. It would be wonderful to fly wherever I wanted! Or would it? Where would I fly? Into the wilderness?

I looked out beyond the oval to a line of magnolia trees by the roadside. They were bold with brilliant rose blossoms. Red and yellow finches, rare for the time of year, were hopping and chirping amongst the leaves. Beautiful. But I could not see past the trees. Didn't I need to know what was behind them?

I turned back to the oval. It was neat and clearly marked. You could see where you had to be if you wanted to score a goal. You could see all around. No surprises. No fears. A little universe marked out and understood.

* * *

The figure of Father Leonard commanded the pulpit. He was dark skinned and burly, the product of some windswept Otago valley. His thinning hair was jet black. He was overweight but not obese, and had the appearance of being much older than he was. He was probably in his mid forties.

'These days it is considered backward to speak critically on the topic I've chosen,' he began in a low boom. 'The Church is, of course, considered medieval and *uncool*.' A few sycophants tittered. 'But my dear brethren,' he continued, 'the Church must uphold the dignity of the human person which, as our Holy Father constantly teaches, is in our *reason*. We are created in the image of God. God is reason. To act according to reason is to act in accordance with the will of the creator. Is it reasonable to murder? To steal? To commit adultery? To lie? It is not. We do not do it. It is against the will of God. Simple? I think so.'

He paused and grasped the edges of the pulpit. He looked hard at his congregation. 'It follows then that anything which perverts reason is against the will of God. What perverts reason? The abuse of alcohol. Drugs. Excessive stimulation of the senses. And dancing. Dancing? But dancing is fun, Father! Yes, it ought to be fun. But if we make it an occasion of sin, it is not fun I tell you. If you could hear the tears of young girls who have confessed to me after a "night of fun".

'Now dancing can be a good thing. It provides relaxation. It teaches us social graces. Here at our school we teach those fine ballroom dances. It teaches our young folk to be ladies and gentlemen. Sometimes though, the passion and pleasure induced by dancing can get the better of us. You *all* know what I'm talking about so I will not spell it out. Prolonging a pleasure, which in itself is good, may turn it into an evil. We may well indulge in some of these modern dances, which are very popular. These are immodest, to use a word I am not ashamed of. *Master* pleasure in order to master yourselves.'

He then went on to speak on the evils of alcoholism. I turned to Angela who was sitting beside me. Her head was slightly bowed. Her eyes were lowered and her lips fallen. I looked to the altar and the crucifix, the plaster image of a bleeding God. I reflected on my life and told myself, *I'm going to learn to dance*.

* * *

The following Saturday I went to Angela's rented house. It was a small but sturdy building facing the grey beach and pounding surf. As I half expected, she surrounded herself with beautiful things: sky blue wallpaper with floral designs; a jar of licorice allsorts and another for jellybeans; a bright blue tin kettle and a Persian cat called Excelsior.

She put on a CD and encouraged me to move with the music. 'Dance is about expressing who you are,' she said. 'You're not rigid, don't dance like you are.'

'But I don't know who I am.'

'Well, we're about to find out.'

During the following weeks I made progress, providing amusement for Excelsior along the way. I began to enjoy myself and I learned a lot about the stranger that was me. And I liked him.

Angela and I started to go to nightclubs. We also went to clifftops to feel the wind. We swam in the river at midnight. We waved to Wanganui and the world beyond from the top of Gonville Hill. She led me through the magnolias. Sometimes what was behind them was more beautiful than they were. Sometimes it was harsh and vile. But whatever it was, it was real. I began to love the world for that.

One Saturday morning I went to Angela's place. We were going to go shopping together.

'Hello Andrew,' she said.

'You're not happy! What's wrong?'

She handed me a letter. It was from the school principal. The blackest paragraph read:

> I have tried on various occasions to remind you that your views on dance do not reflect the teachings of the Catholic Church. You are teaching in a Catholic school and so are reasonably expected to conform to certain doctrinal standards, even if you do not agree with them. Since you will not heed my advice I must regrettably allow you to seek other employment.

'Angela, I'm sorry.'

'I love those kids.' She held me.

That night I went to Gonville. The moon was full. The finished wall stood before me. It glared at me. I glared at it. Twenty minutes later a police car passed by. They saw a can lying on the pavement and me dancing on top of the wall. On it were huge bold letters that read THEY WILL NEVER MASTER THE DANCE.

* * *

The cell door clanged open. 'Angela!' I said.

She walked in. She smiled. 'I saw the wall.'

The door shut.

'I hate them,' I said.

'Don't hate them. But I'm glad you did it. Thank you.'

I clasped her hands in mine. 'You've redeemed me.'

'No Andrew. You redeemed yourself.'

We were silent and then she said, 'I'm going to leave Wanganui. There's a studio in Wellington wanting an instructor. They asked a month ago. I turned them down, but now ... '

'Do you have to go?'

'I will miss the children. And you, Andrew.'

'Angela, I ... '

'Andrew, don't say it.'

'Why not?'

'Because it's not me you love. It's the dance. And you have it. You have it more than anyone I've known.'

I began to cry. So did Angela.

'You don't need me any more,' she said.

The door opened. A policeman stepped in. 'Father Leonard isn't pressing charges,' he said. 'So you're free to go.'

Angela held both my hands. Then she released them and extended one arm toward the open door. 'You're free,' she said.

I smelled something as we parted outside the station. I think it was magnolias.

Faraway

I send words through this muddy sphere
Not returning, wailing, flailing
Toward some pest ridden shadow, dying.
Barren silence returning, firing
The vacant vaults with mournful scorn.

One note may yet reach a distant bough,
And colouring realms by its richness
Call me through the void.
It knows me. It is me devoid
Of the cynicism that is my light
And I wish was not
Here in the land they call real.
There I live. Here I die.
Torn, I hope and love and lie.

First Love

I made a cage
Full of leaden gods
Which shut the view.

I ate my waste
I drank my sighs.
This was grace to me.

Forgive me.
I have kept you
From the air.

But now
I will keep bees
And feed on jelly

Until I am no more.

And there is only you.

You will sing
And laugh
And dance
And shed warm tears
Like a lover.

You will be mother and father
To the universe.

Nicky Graban

White House, White Moon

She stared back, motionless. Had cried the rivers before, but tonight her hollow eyes were empty, her throat paralysed. Jude watched as he threw some clothes into a suitcase and strode towards the door. He briefly stopped and turned to aim one more dart. 'And yes, you're right about one thing. I have been seeing someone else. Who'd blame me?' The heavy door slammed. Peace moved into the house, a companion she could hold dear.

Jude spent the rest of that night methodically moving her things from the double bedroom into the downstairs spare room. Six-year-old Jack hadn't woken through any of the noise, surprisingly. He was usually a light sleeper. Jude shed her clothes. As she lay naked on the single bed her pale body prickled in the cold air. She enjoyed the sensation, and didn't seek warmth. Discomfort suited her at this moment, gave her a sense of strength. As she waited patiently for a hint of sunrise she was powerless to stop her mind swimming to dangerous places. Insanity was breathing in her face. But the whisper had been right in its advice. Peter was having an affair, and she cared for the strangest reasons.

She wrapped her arms tightly around her bare breasts, providing affection from someone she could trust. At the age of thirty-two her dreams were lost. The shimmering images of hope once reflected in her eyes now vaporised, leaving an empty glare. Foolish images anyway. They were never shared, and never materialised. In this house two plus one had never equalled three. She decided the room definitely needed painting. White.

Jack exploded into the new day with vigour. He seemed not to notice when people disappeared from his day, so this was like any other. It was when they appeared, when they invaded his picture that he grew anxious and took to chewing on toys until his gums bled. As Jude had expected, his world continued to revolve around the sun, stars and moon. His obsession with all things astronomical was his protective wall. Jude's world became Jack, the sole parent pension, and loneliness.

'Counselling will help,' the doctor had advised when Jude arrived for her prescription.

The counsellor, twenty-two year old Rochelle Sheldon, discovered problems Jude never knew she had. That was helpful. In the way of extending the counselling sessions and increasing her intake of medication. Very productive, from a therapeutic perspective. Gave her plenty more to think about. Like why she was still struggling with the fact that her son had autism.

'How did Jack's diagnosis of autism affect your marriage, your husband?'

'Maybe it's the autism he's been running away from?'

'A marriage is like a garden that needs tending, and with Jack demanding so much of your time it must be hard to give Peter much attention?'

Jude found it difficult to answer, to even speak. Anger was an emotion she had become expert at controlling and she was thankful for that now.

She arrived home after her therapy session to find a truck parked in the driveway of her house.

'Mrs Thompson?'

'Yes.'

'We're here for the television, video and computer. You would have been notified of the repossession by mail.'

'No, I know nothing about this. My husband has been making the payments regularly. Hasn't he?'

'Apparently not. Here's a copy of the last letter.' He handed her the papers.

Jude opened the door and sat, confused. Within minutes she was staring at the dusty corner of the lounge room. She vacuumed the empty corner, and continued through the house until her mother arrived with Jack a few hours later. As Jude scrubbed her hands in the bathroom her mother looked in. Jude prepared herself.

'Maybe he'd be better behaved if he got out more often, Jude?' Jack spun through the house checking each room, like a tornado slamming each door. Finished, he sat curled in foetal position where the television had been, hands covering his eyes, panting, rocking back and forth, groaning.

* * *

Three months later the four-bedroom house shone white, inside and out. But it still felt unkempt, run-down, dirty.

Jude learned a lot about herself in those months, no thanks to therapy. Scrubbing carpets and bleaching tiles opened new possibilities for her. But Rochelle Sheldon had unknowingly taught Jude something useful that day. The skill of assertiveness. Enough to cancel all further counselling appointments anyway.

A routine settled on them. Weekdays Jack was taxied to and from the special school and Jude enveloped herself in work on the house. Cleaning and painting. Saturday nights Jude studied Jack's world from her fraying cane chair on the back verandah. The irritating squeak, squeak, squeak, provided peace for Jack. The rhythm of the swing was relaxing. Hypnotically soothing. Thick locks of black hair hung limply over his eyes. He hated haircuts so she rarely bothered. His upward gaze seemed to pass right through the stars, to transport him to a place she didn't know and he couldn't tell her of.

Jude stood for a better view of the black clouds hovering nearby. They made a habit of crashing in and exploding at the last moment. Standing also allowed her a glance at the neighbour, the purple-haired old woman whose favourite pass-time was to spy through the gaps in the fence. The rain would hold off a little longer tonight. The old woman probably would too.

The telephone rang abruptly. Jude rose and stepped inside, her movements slow and laborious.

'Hello Mrs Thompson, it's Sally here,' sung the girl who was paid by a government department to take Jack out once a month. 'I'm sorry but I've come down with a terrible flu and I wondered if I could change my day with Jack. I could take him out next Sunday instead of tomorrow, if that's okay?'

Back outside Jack continued to squeak. Jude's weight sunk again into the old chair, her frame comforted a little by the familiar cushions. Tears glistened and trickled. Questions burdened her mind, suffocating every breath. A myriad of answers swayed back and forth, a pendulum alive inside. When the tide of darkness was complete, Jude prepared to face another night.

'Time to go inside Jack,' she spoke gently.

He shook his head violently and his hands gripped the cold chains. 'No, no, no, no … ' his high-pitched scream rang out.

'Come on Jack, it's tea time and we're having your favourite noodles tonight.' Plain boiled pasta. That, together with bananas and Weet-bix, was one of the few foods he'd allow into his mouth.

Jack's body fell onto the lawn as Jude tried to move him into the house. He kicked and screamed. The old woman's face peered at them through the fence. Jude's stomach knotted with pain. She sat on the lawn and rubbed her son's body hoping to bring calm. Jack's body quivered with fear, his eyes squeezed tight in an effort to shut out the world. Jude pressed his little body against hers and eventually peace came. She lifted him into her arms and carried him inside to the lounge where he could watch the old television.

Jude began running the bath and preparing tea. Her only child, the baby who was to solidify the marriage. The joy of birth, the gift of life, all that. Age one, diagnosis hyperactive … age two, developmentally delayed … age three, autism … age six divorce and medication for two.

As steam began to fill the bathroom Jude saw her reflection in the mirror. She stared into the round sockets questioningly. Black bags told her story, together with cheeks that hadn't felt laughter for too long. Loneliness, isolation. Self imposed? Partly. Her eyes fell to the bottles in the bathroom cabinet. *Judith Thompson* on some, *Jack Thompson* on others. No light stuff here, heavy doses required. Her hand reached out and collected two of the near full bottles.

The telephone rang again. Passing the lounge room door, Jude noticed Jack lying still next to the television, squashing a worn out cow in his arms. With hesitation Jude answered the phone.

'Hello?' her tired voice answered. Sounding 'normal' now required too much effort.

'Hi Jude. How are you feeling today?' It was Mum. (How *depressed* are you feeling today?)

'I'm okay Mum.'

'I'm just calling to see whether you want me to pick you up for the wedding tomorrow or are you going to drive there yourself?'

'There's a problem. Jack's carer has cancelled.'

'Oh.'

Shrill squealing ended the conversation, Jack's timing perfect. A hundred feet pounded the kitchen floorboards, circling with knees bouncing high. Arms flapped in an effort to fly. The eruption of noise was painful, even for Jack. His angel face grimaced, and dark eyes shone fearfully.

'Moon, moon, moon, moon, moon … ' was endlessly demanded. Jude suspected her son was part werewolf.

'I'll take you to the moon Jack.'

'Moon, moon, moon … ' he continued. They lay on their backs together in his dark bedroom, moon and star stickers glowing on the ceiling above.

Later came the scotch.

Autism made the rules in this house. Jude had coped with her altered version of life only because of the support she'd found. In scotch and pills. More understanding than people.

Back in her chair on the verandah, Jude watched the dark clouds pass magically over the white moon. She understood the beauty Jack saw in it, but no more. Her body was freezing and her mind trapped.

Peter's concerned face appeared at the back door. One of his more frequently used masks these days.

'I knocked Jude, but you mustn't have heard from out here. Aren't you cold?'

Heartbeats pounded, one with anger, the other with fear.

'No, I didn't hear you.'

'Your mum phoned me. I can have Jack tomorrow if you want to go to the wedding.' He sat uncomfortably on the edge of a chair.

'I'm putting the house up for sale. It's falling apart.' Jude got her lie in before he had a chance, and she gathered strength from this. She threw rejection at him as often as opportunity allowed. And unexpectedly he'd made her decision for her tonight.

The noise of Peter's car leaving pulled Jack from his sleep into screams of fear. In love with the universe but afraid of the dark. Jude lay beside him whispering and pointing to the Milky Way on the ceiling. She brought comfort, and his pills. Ready for sleep, she swallowed hers too. They lay together in the white room looking at the moon and waiting for the medication to take effect. She felt his thick black hair against her cheek as their breathing slowed and autism left the house.

Ethiopian Mother

Beside the tukul
'*Enkwandehna metah chu*'
she welcomes
white smile,
standing tall in the doorway
'I am Itenesh'
You are my sister.

She travels the road
Carting sticks with a mule
hunched back, high load
Heart is heavy for you
Lost son.

One world but so vast
The distance immense
She imagines she's there
and she is in a sense;
Brown baby.

Clean eucalypt perfume
Wafts her nose as yours,
And mountainous ranges
surround both the lands.
He grows.

Brown eyes see you
And shine with tears,
reach into your home
and watch all that you do
'God has blessed you my son'
There is purpose in this,
She believes.

Though traditions are lost
you will hold your head high
Like the lion,
be a strong and proud leader
As your name loud
she cries.

Little Ones

Smile so sincere, eyes dance and shine,
so divine
Cheeks bursting with happiness
'Mum Mum Mum' desperately called
Standing on tippy toes now
Impatiently
Longingly
Looks at me then the tub
Naked body is tense, the excitement runs through
me too
Every nerve
Every muscle
All singing in tune

When the water's just right,
and taps are turned off
His toes begin dancing,
the impatience is rising
until finally feet become wet

And now in the water, his hands slap with glee
Hey watch me!
Water splashes with giggles
Magically
Delightfully
Pale skin, blue eyes just like mine
Chubby legs, wrinkled bottom
Red hair wispy fine
The circles rippling wider as thoughts in my mind
Little things,
Little ones
Bring full circle to meet
And spiral on.

Merlin to his love Nimue

Still I lie imprisoned in this cold cave
Rich with endless time! For, my love I gave
You all – not just my heart but magic too.
And with this power my trust in you who

Stole from the Light to conjure this Dark end
A silence eternal, no love to tend.
And I with Sight knew tragedy would come
Yet still I yearned your love, my senses numb.

Was I a fool, or after all a man
As well as the great wizard that I am!
I laugh of course, how great was I to need
A woman who would do this evil deed?

You knew of all my legendary quests
With Uther then Arthur we passed all tests,
Faced dragons, sought the Grail, always able
Our courage and strength bore the Round Table.

All this and more was my life dear Nimue
As wood goddess rode to Camelot, you
Learned from this wizard all Craft that was Good,
Grew tired, entombed me with rocks in the wood.

The air here is thick, the smell foul to breathe
Only your sympathy could bring my leave
I wonder, is this death who looks on me
Or is it madness from beneath I see?

For here I lie trapped, the Stone of Merlin
My time is gone, and the power within.

Scotch Whisky

Dust on his shoulders,
Red bottle on show.
White label turned yellow,
Gold letters that glow.

His value's unknown,
Just too high to say.
The spirit sits safely
To see the next day.

He's travelled the world,
Improved with age.
Is now at his peak
And feels safe on his stage.

Then disaster one day
With marriage declared,
The bottle's cracked open,
The gold liquid is shared.

Crystal glasses are raised,
They clink with a cheer.
Until round by round,
All intentions are clear.

Bagpipes are heard
As the level drops down,
And sweet sadness unfolds
As he remembers hometown.

For this whisky he knows
Will be talked of for years,
To be brought up again
All humbled with tears.

Tim Earl

The Big Smoke

David

There is a pale outline of my face reflected in the dusty glass. The muted kaluck-kaluck kaluck-kaluck of the train is relentless. I gaze absent-mindedly out the window. Fences and dirt tracks divide the landscape into geometric patterns. Here and there a tree, or a row of trees, punctures the otherwise unbroken quilt of yellow brown. It must be months since Winnatunga council area has had rain. Up above, the wires go along and then move up and down suddenly as a telegraph pole whizzes past. There are five wires, like a music stave. I imagine notes placed on the wires and in the gaps in between them. Kaluck-kaluck, kaluck-kaluck, kaluck-kaluck, kaluck-kaluck.

Surely the novel I'm reading is more interesting than what's outside the window. I deliberately return my attention to the page in front of me. 'Lead on! Cried Manfred. I will follow thee to the Gulf of Perdition. The spectre marched sedately ... '

I awake for no reason in particular and shift in the seat, which has become uncomfortable again. The seat next to me is empty. The talkative butcher who sat there is probably still up ahead in the saloon car at the bar. The book has fallen to the floor at my feet. We must be nearly there now. I pick up the book and stand to grab the backpack from the rack overhead, carefully so as not to lose balance. The train has slowed though. It is way to slow, almost walking pace. Something must be wrong. I put the book away and sit down again on the green cloth seat.

The landscape is still yellow-brown but then it changes. A line approaches, beyond which all is black. The Gulf of

Perdition. The sparse trees are black with light brown leaves. Many don't even have leaves and smoke rises from some of these. We pass a log, black and ashen-grey. It has caved in on one side and an orange flame haunts its charred skeleton. Like Walpole's spectre, the train rolls sedately through the surreal landscape.

Jacob

Tomorrow David comes home on the train he does. On Sunday is Palm Sunday when Jesus rided on the donkey but tomorrow David rides on the train. There's David in the bible too but he doesn't ride on the train he doesn't. Jesus doesn't ride on the train neither but David my brother does. David's my brother he is. Not David in the bible but the other David he's my brother he is.

'C'mon Jake,' Toby says. 'Let's go up to the shearing shed on the motorbike.' Toby's my brother too he is and Hannah is my sister. I like the motorbike 'cause it goes round and round like the train. We can see the train in the shed in the upstairs we can – the train that David rides in. David's my brother too.

'Where are they?' says Hannah and Toby says he doesn't know and Mummy says stop it so we go we do.

Hannah

This is like the worst day of my life it is. Like I thought Trudy was a friend a good friend like basically the best and now she's going out with Peter who she knows I like 'cause I told her yesterday. She didn't even wait till I had asked him out first and now it's holidays so they'll spend heaps of time with each other and now I can't find my smokes anywhere and right now I really need one. I bet Toby's got them. I'll bet he nicked them again the little shit.

'Toby!' I call him from where I am in my room. 'Toby, where are they?'

'I don't know,' he says but he does know where they are, I know he does.

'Toby!'

'Stop it you two!' calls Mum. 'Tobias Sepson if you've taken something of Hannah's, give it back now!'

'I haven't. I swear I haven't. C'mon Jake let's go for a bike ride.' I open the bedroom door so I can catch them before they go but they're gone already. I hear the buzz of the trail bike engine so I run outside to catch them but it's too late. Toby goes hooning up to the old shearing shed with Jake clinging on behind him. So I decide to walk there which sucks because it's a really hot day.

The old shearing shed is massive and has two stories. It's where Toby went last time he stole my smokes because he can go to the upstairs part and just sit there and smoke and no-one can see him but he can see through the gaps in the walls if anyone comes up from the house.

This heat sucks. I hate days like this when it's hot and the wind keeps blowing dust into your face. Trudy is a bitch and I never want to talk to her again.

I'm not far from the shed now but to get in I have to walk around the other side past where the petrol pump is and then climb up the hay-baler to the top story. The shed is a big ugly metal box that stands next to the track that runs along the edge of our property where it borders with the McPherson's. I hear the trail bike again and Toby and Jake come along the track toward me so I step in front of them and make them stop.

'Well, hand them over you little twerp,' I say to Toby. He just sits there on the bike and doesn't say anything and doesn't look at me. Then little Jake starts crying loudly over the noise of the trail bike motor and I notice that he looks kind of ill, sort of a pale green colour.

'You idiot Toby! Why'd you give them to him for? He's too young,' I say.

'We got more important things to worry 'bout now.' Toby revs the engine and they get past me and take off down the track towards the house. At first I think they're just conning me but then I catch a whiff of something bad, real bad. Like something you just don't want to smell on a day like today with the weather being the way it is. I can hear it too now –

it's in the shed. It's like a low pitch muffled roar with crackles in it. As I'm looking at the shed, the whole of the wall collapses with a metallic screech and is replaced by a wall of orange.

It's a beautiful thing, fire is. I love the way flames dance over and on top of one another. The shed looks like one of them weird modern art paintings, like abstract expression or something. Suddenly I remember the petrol tank and I begin running back down to the house. My school shoes aren't comfortable for running but at least I'm not wearing my platforms. At the house Mum is herding Jake and Toby into the car.

'C'mon!' she calls to me, waving her arm energetically.

Bill

'Well Mr Spock,' I say, 'I reckon we must have fixed it this time. What do you reckon?' Spock barks and wags his tail, enthusiastic as usual. I take me hat off and wipe me brow. Yep, I sure hope it's fixed now. Third attempt this is, so I sure hope I've fixed it this time. I drink some water out of the bottle and give a bit to Spock too. Don't like working in this heat but it has to be done otherwise the crops'll fail.

'Here we go, Spock,' I say and then flip the ignition switch. The whole pump shudders and then comes to life with a chug-chug-chug-chug. The pump shaft arm comes up with a grinding noise but then stops mid-cycle. The whole damn machine starts shuddering and making spluttering noises and then it just stops altogether and I'm sure I can smell burning so I turn it off at the switch. Spock knows what this means, 'cause he starts whining.

'Yep, I guess I'll just have to call someone in from outside.' I've a good mind to kick the ugly contraption but I know that it won't fix it 'cause it never does. Besides, I kicked it already today after the second time I fixed it and it still wouldn't work. I pack up the tools into the kit and put it on the back of the tractor. Spock jumps aboard too 'cause he knows we're leaving now and I have to get someone else to fix the bore pump so the lucerne can stay alive in this heat. Damn shame it wouldn't work for me 'cause every mechanic around here charges like a wounded bull these days. And most likely they're all busy now 'cause it's nearly Easter and they're always busy around holiday season. This could put us in a bit of a fix right now, unless there's some rain on the way. That won't be today though. The sky is brown with dust. The sun is low in the sky but it is more orange than normal on account of the dust.

I start up the old tractor and thank the Lord it still works when you want it to. I head back toward the house along the track by the McPherson's place. Spock is still whining all the time but I keep telling him we'll get someone to fix it then everything will be all right. I must have really done some damage this time though, 'cause I'm sure I can still smell it. But then I get a bad feeling about it all, what with that dog whining and the weird weather …

As I get to the top of the hill I see a most hellish sight. It's as if the sun has leaked on to the ground up ahead 'cause both the flames and the sun above them are the same shade of orange. And the sky is turning dark. Looks like the way ahead is completely blocked and what's more the wind is blowing this way. I put me hand up to shield me eyes 'cause that heat is blowing straight at me. Now I know what it is I could smell and why Mr Spock is whimpering and whining. I turn the tractor with a three-point turn, trust Ruth and the kids into the Lord's care, and head in the other direction 'cause I know with this wind it won't take long for that fire to catch me. I figure the best thing to do is to go and see McPherson and ask for his help. I'll take a shortcut across his paddock on the left and go straight over the hill to his house. I have the tool kit with me so it wouldn't take much to cut through the fence so I can take the tractor through.

McPherson

'Where's me binoculars, darl?' I say. Gloria doesn't turn to look at me but just keeps watchin' that dust cloud. At fifty-three she's still as good-looking as when I married her.

'You sold them dear, remember?' she says.

I remember now. I should'a asked more than twenty bucks

for them binoculars. They were a good set. The rifle has a telescopic sight. I go inside the house to get it. When I return to the porch, Gloria gives me a funny look like as if to reproach me for bein' about to shoot somebody.

'What?' I say. 'It's got a telescopic sight. It's just as good as any set of binoculars. And I haven't even taken it out of the case yet.'

'Well I don't think you even need to use binoculars to see what's happening over there. Look!' she says, so I look to where she's pointing.

'Struth.' It's Sepson, or at least it's his old red tractor. He seems to be heading this way, toward the gate. No wonder that bull's havin' a fit. There's so much dust in the air that I'm guessing that Oscar is right behind him, chasin' him.

That Sepson family is a weird mob. Specially their eldest one that always wears black and plays violin. And now he's gone to the big smoke to learn to play it some more. What sort of life is that for a young man? And that girl that doesn't wear much except in winter and always tells fibs! Some folk oughta be ashamed the way they bring their kids up these days. Still, Sepson must have some brains. He sold all his sheep early on and planted lucerne and everyone says there's money in that. What's he think he's doin' driving his tractor through my paddock? I open the case and take the rifle out.

'Be careful love,' says Gloria.

'It's awright darl, I never keep any bullets in this thing.' I hold it up to me shoulder and look through the sight. I never seen Bill Sepson look so sweated up and panicked all the years I've known him. I still can't see how far Oscar is behind him. I know he's there though. There ain't nothing that make a man run for his life like that, except bein' chased by a mad bull.

Suddenly the tractor is sliding and slipping all over the place and I figure that Oscar must've hit him from behind. The tractor disappears in the cloud of dust then shoots out at a different angle and I can see Sepson still hanging on. And there is Oscar, an angry shadow, right behind him. They're side-on to us now so I can see them better but Sepson is try-ing to swing around toward the gate with not far to go now.

He leaps off the tractor and hits the ground running – running toward the gate. I didn't know a fella his age could run so fast. The tractor hits a pothole or something 'cause it flips and rolls over a few times before coming to a stop. Oscar pulls up halfway between Sepson and the tractor and looks from one to the other as if he can't make up his mind which to charge at. Sepson reaches the gate and scrambles over the top.

'I reckon I better take the ute and go over there and find out what the hell Sepson's doing driving a bloody tractor through our bloody paddock and stirring up our bull like that,' I say.

'Ted.' There is concern in Gloria's voice.

'It's awright, I won't take this with me.' I lower the gun.

'No Ted, look!' I look to where she points. Above the treetops on the far side of the paddock hangs a long cloud of smoke.

'Struth!' I can smell it now too, smell it in the air. 'You'd better go in and call the CFS, darl. I'm takin' the ute to pick up Sepson.'

Ruth

'I see there's been a fire,' David says. Jacob starts to cry.

'Hush,' says Hannah. She comforts him crouching down to his level and placing her arm around his shoulders. We put David's suitcase and violin in the back of the old station wagon, in with the chickens. I look around knowing that Mr Spock is still unaccounted for. We wait while we watch the fire front head toward the horizon and I try not to think about Bill.

We then pile in to the station wagon. The car smells, and sounds, like a chicken coop. I drive the car out of the railway station carpark but something doesn't feel right with the steering. I pull over to check the tyres, just in front of the level crossing. One is flat, the front one at the left. We all get out and I make the kids hold the chickens while I take out the wheel lever and the jack.

As I'm loosening the wheel nuts a familiar bark accosts my ears.

'Spock! Spock! Spock! Spock!' calls Jacob. I feel the dog's tongue slobbering all over my face and catch glimpses of that mottled black and grey fur and those pointed ears.

'Toby,' I say. 'Come and get this dog outa my face.' Someone lifts the dog away and I continue with the wheel. I jack up the car, brace the wheel between my knees and remove the wheel nuts. Bells start ringing in my head: ding, ding, ding, ding, ding.

'The train! Train! Train!' says Jacob and I realise the bells are not in my head but it's the wig-wams. Must be the freight train from Broken Hill. I watch the boom gates go down and the red lights flashing and all the time their bells going ding, ding, ding, ding. The train crawls past as I position the new tyre. As the boom gates lift I see McPherson's ute waiting on the other side. The passenger door opens and Bill steps out, squinting into the sun. I stand as he walks towards me, a relieved smile beaming through his sooty face.

Sophia Coopman

Ars Insanity

To understand the landscape of my world, you must hold the paintbrush for yourself. Prepare your own palette. All you need are the cold colours of melancholy …

Step 1:
You will start with a background of grey – blot the colour on without care; darken your canvas. Do not bother rinsing your brush between colours; you are creating a world that blurs, where edges run into edges like dirtied watercolours.

Step 2:
There is no definite distinction between earth and sky. You choose which one is darker. Dot your paintbrush on the ground, colour it in dull browns. Make sure to obstruct it with boulders, jagged rocks that protrude like tumours. If you have an eye for detail, paint in the prickles, the dying stumps of grass, the fallen twigs. Make any form of vegetation decayed, dying.

Step 3:
Dip your paintbrush in water, and make the sky a watery blur. Colour it with dark clouds, impregnated with grief. Further back on your canvas, create bold lines, menacing shadows, so that the impression imposed is one of heavy, sinister clouds tumbling towards you. Paint no sunshine. Remember – blacks, greys, browns are your only colours.

Step 4:
Dip your paintbrush in black, and stroke deadened trees into being. Paint spindly trunks and sharp, protruding branches, jutting out at severe right angles. Twisted, make them tear at

the sky, ripping open the darkened clouds, and bringing down rain as heavy as the collective tears of the multitudes.

Step 5:
Reach for a finer brush; immerse it in a paint darker than the trees. Here you will create the photo never quite developed. Draw outlines of creatures – are they human? Monster? You decide – but leave them out of focus, so you will never really know if they are there or not. Streak your brush, create movement. Draw them crouching behind trees, hiding in branches, spindly creatures, all lines and harsh angles. But never bring them into full vision, so that they forever elude you. Do not colour their eyes; leave a gaping vacancy, so that the omissions demand your full attention, glaringly obvious in the darkness you have painted; leering, watching you.

Step 6:
Put down your paintbrush. Of course, you have left out the cliffs, but those you cannot see until you fall down them, tumbling over the edge like a single unstoppable tear. Now pack up your palette, put down your brush, and step inside the canvas …

*   *   *

Note the chill you couldn't achieve by colouring, the icy breath of a wind that numbs your face, tangles your hair. Had you noticed that your clothes have vanished, or did the realisation suddenly hit you with full force and leave you alone, naked, vulnerable?

Listen to what you could not see – the endless whispering of the wind; is it calling your name, over and over … ? There is nothing else to listen for, except the fall of your own footsteps, the monotonous thud as your feet bear down on the deadened ground. The occasional snap of a twig. And no matter how hard you try, you will never discern *their* footfall. You will only feel them, feel them watching you with razor eyes, peeling you down to your final skin.

The ground is hard beneath your bare feet. Cracking,

zigzagged with jagged lines that run for miles, the path you tread is dangerous, and prickles stick to your skin like dried blood.

Don't stand for too long. It seems I missed my pass out, and am destined to wish for straight lines while I travel in circles. I have fallen down the cliffs many times, but always woken up back where I started. Hurt, weary, and weaker than before, but alive and behind the same starting line.

Be sure to step out of the canvas while your can! Hang it up on your wall. Take a step back and tilt your head to the side. And tell me, Doc, what do you think? Is there a way out?

Blackwood Station, 9:00 AM

You are there every morning,
more reliable than the bus that
takes me away
from you.

I know
that when I turn the corner
you will be sitting -
slightly off centre-
on the wooden bench,
your hands in a lap of faded denim,
feet planted firmly
side by side, head
tucked snugly into your collarbone.

At first I thought you were praying,
now I know
that you watch us
silently, objectively.

You will be wearing the same
tattered shirt
and sometimes you will rub the left cuff,
worn with the attention of fingertips,
faded, fraying.
The same jeans will hang from you -
old, shabby, ripped
and offering memories I will perhaps never know;
a faded, dying testament of your travels.
They tell me you have painted,
walked in muddy fields,
and failed to change your pants in over three months.

I will look at your same boots,
cracking, caked with hardened mud
and wonder
where they have been.
And next to them, there will always
be the bag
resting patiently, a faithful dog.
You enjoy the mastery,
stroking it lovingly,
opening and closing its pockets, its metal teeth.

Each day you examine me, your eyes all question.
I hope I can give the answers you so
discreetly,
so innocently
search for. Your journey
starts at my feet, ends at my collarbone.
And no matter what I am wearing,
what I am doing,
there is always acceptance in your eyes.

You are ever curious,
your eyes flitting like butterflies, fascinated
by the people around you.
I see you mimic them;

your head bobbing like the
daily jogger's,
your fingers extending,
then retracting into a fist
like the man next to you.
I see you smile at your body
and its borrowed functions,
I see you smile at
all who walk by.

You observe all conversation
and repeat it back
silently
and to nobody.

You will look at your watch,
and stand at the same time each morning;
each morning I hope that the bus comes on time,
that your faith in your world won't be rocked,
that you won't have to sit back down,
your downcast face nestling confusion
and intangible expectations.

In a world drowning in change,
you are like clockwork.
And you do not understand when they
let you down.

But when the bus does come,
and you
and your faithful bag rise,
you will take the second seat from the back,
open the window
and expose the raucous laughter, the fun,
the sometimes animalistic sounds.
Here, you will
break out in a smile,
so touching in its intensity,

authenticity
and your stick-thin arms
will hang from the window
waving vigorously,
your lips sounding an affectionate 'goodbye'.

And I will watch you depart
and board my own bus
where I will be met by hostile stares,
by silence,
emptiness,
where I will appreciate your honesty,
your innocence
even more.
Here I will cherish your rarity,
the being you remain true to.
And here, without you,
I will realise that in just one smile
you can give me more
than a whole bus filled
with my people, filled with falsity.

Katherine Doube

A head for numbers

A head for numbers,
    that's what she says she hasn't got.
She also says
    she doesn't understand all this modern stuff,
    that she'll leave it to the young ones.
She asked me five times
    last time I saw her
what I was doing now.
    Still at school?
           no.
    Work?
          yes.
               also uni.
    right …
    when she was young …

When she was young,
    things were different.
She lived on the farm.
She'd get up at 5 to milk the cows before school,
    she can't stand milk now,
    it's the smell that puts her off.
She left school at 14,
    she had to help her parents in the shop.
Their winery shop.
    She sold wine.
She'd hear 'experts' speak of the oak undertones,
    about premium fruit picked at optimum ripeness.
She's done that her whole life,
    worked with money
             with people
             with wine.

She doesn't have a head for numbers.
She can't remember her grand-daughters name.
She scoffs whenever she hears someone mention the
     complex flavour of a wine.

but she laughs
     and smiles
                    and maybe that is enough.

Suburban contrast

In this suburb
     the Saturdays are quiet.
The mowing is done during the week
     when the owners are at work
     and can't be given migraines from the noise
                    (and from the pill-and-champagne mix from
                    the night before).
Some might call it peaceful.
Others would point out the dull bored eyes in the houses,
     the intercoms and tight security fences,
                    high and electric.
Others would point out the garbage bins full of bottles
     and the single serve take out
                    delivered to nine bedroom houses.
Some might see the big houses
                    and shiny cars
     and sigh wistfully as they drive past
with their kids laughing and screaming in the back
on their way to a barely affordable holiday.

Could have

She stands at the dirty window and stares past the
    splintered frame.
Out into the past
    or the future.
Into the life she once had,
    the life she could have had,
    the life she wants.
She sees lost opportunities drift past on clouds,
    high prestige jobs snatched up by the better
      and more worthy,
    more successful (impressive) boyfriends wander
      past in the rain,
missed careers,
missed passions.
A life she could have had.

Insect

A Flash.
Orange, yellow, green
reflect off iridescent armour.
The vein filled wings are still
    watching, waiting.
An image of complete indestructibility.
                        (squash)

Old men

Old men in wrinkled cardigans,
    dull, neutral colours
        fading into the background
        fading into death.
Wearing earthy colours
    so as to fit in 3 months later
            6 feet under.

Some days are diamonds

Some days are diamonds
she said to me
up to her arms in flour.

Did she notice the days pass
grey after grey,
I never saw a sparkle.

But she insisted
that some days were diamonds
though she never showed them to me.

Lise Mackie

Polish

In the old wooden cot by the bed, a sleepy head slowly shows itself over the battered rail that three children had teethed upon. The frayed cotton sheet that had covered him was tangled around his feet. Rubbing sleep from his eyes, James slowly begins his early morning grizzling. My husband lies heavily beside me. I ease back the cotton cover and slide my feet onto the carpet noticing with delight the flash of scarlet red polish on my toenails. Time allowed me to paint them last night. Stroking the brilliant red over my nails gave me such pleasure, livening up my spirits as well as my feet. The summer's day was dawning with the prospect of strappy sandals!

I lifted James from his cot without lowering the side – a twinge in my back told me I shouldn't have. At 2 years old, he is getting quite heavy. Wearily I padded out to the lounge and sat James on a chair, clutching his one-eyed teddy bear. I went into the kitchen and, giving James a biscuit to keep him quiet, put the kettle on for the coffee needed to wake me up. The aroma burst from the granules as I poured the steaming water into my cup. I take a deep breath, enjoying the fragrance, and instinctively wrap my hands around it, as if to warm them. I sit with James in the lounge and we have a cuddle. No one else is awake. The flat is shrouded in silence, and the fluorescent tube from the kitchen glowing through the doorway is our only light. I show James my toenails – I can tell he's impressed!

Claire wakes soon after. Although it is school holidays, she is used to getting up and getting ready by herself. She wanders out to get a drink, stopping to plant a kiss on her brother's head. James smiles adoringly at his big sister. Claire is like another mother to him. At only six, she is a very responsible child. I remember clearly when she was born, her steel grey eyes barely seeing and her tuft of blond hair sticking up from her head. She was a beautiful baby and hardly ever cried. I flash my toenails at her. With awe in her face, she begs to have her nails painted also.

By breakfast time, the sunlight is streaming in the kitchen window. It is going to be a hot day. Robert padded out quietly and said his good-mornings – none of the 4-year-old's energy of last night apparent. The stainless steel sink caught chunks of light and flashed them up into my face, making me squint. I poured coffee into Dean's favourite mug and Claire took it to him in our bedroom. This is their special time – it has been since she was a baby. Dean dotes on Claire and she thinks the world of him. He has a great relationship with all of our children. Rough and tumble time in the evening is a ritual with the boys. I call out from the kitchen that it is getting late. Dean has a shower and hurriedly dresses. Then, with cries of goodbye, he leaves for work.

My day continues as it does everyday, with the exception of taking Claire to school. Guiltily I plant the children in a row in front of the T.V. so I can make the beds and wash the dishes. They sit there looking like daffodils, with the sun reflecting off their blond heads, each one a little taller than the one next to it.

With the blazing sun past its midday mark, it became apparent the children would not settle down for a nap. Robert fights weariness, condemning it as a baby's tendency. Claire is a great help and will settle down to read when the little ones are asleep. My few hours of contemplation (and housework) will be delayed yet again. The tiny flat seems littered with bodies as children and toys loll on the floor. Fingerprints of jam smear the coffee table. The frustration of the inescapable heat and whining children is more than I can bear. The only salvation for my sanity would be to take them out and tire them so that sleep would come from exhaustion. I gather James into my arms and, turning my back on the turmoil, usher the other two out of the door. Slamming it shut behind me, I turned the key and slipped it in my pocket.

The darkened hallway was cooler but smelled of dampness and stale sweat. The two older children were jumping excitedly at the prospect of going to the park, escaping the confines and boredom of home.

At the first sign of freedom, Robert made a break and left me struggling with the door, shouting like a fishwife for him to come back. Claire managed to round him up with the skill of a rodeo rider and, under threat of dire consequences, we made our way down Thurston St. without any more incidents.

Wishing I had remembered the pusher, I shifted James from one hip to the other.

Memorial Park is an oasis in a dessert of council flats. Concrete paths dissect its patchy green grass. Lovers sometimes stroll here – always in danger of being hit by a ten year old on a bike. Raucous teenagers meet here, craving the space and freedom not possible at home. Thankful for the shady Plane tree that casts a dappled shade over the bench, I wearily sit down. The wooden slats feel rough through my thin floral dress and I caress the brass plaque embedded in the second rung of timber, wondering about the lives of the family who donated this place of rest to the city. They lived in the area before all the flats were built. I imagine them here when the roads were only dirt tracks. The ramshackle homestead overlooking the park belonged to them – now it belongs to the council and is a shelter for the homeless.

Claire and Robert race over to the gaudy plastic play equipment and immediately begin to argue over who will have first turn on the swing. In typical two-year-old style, James has found some dirt to play in and is filthy within a minute. Deciding to relax and not let it worry me, I ease back onto the seat – the fresh air reviving my flagging spirits.

A shrill scream from the swings tells me the argument has not been resolved. Claire runs to me shouting, 'He bit me, he bit me!' and is eager to show me the evidence. Robert comes swiftly to plead his innocence. Scalding Robert for biting, I turn my attention to Claire. Tears well in her eyes as we inspect the red imprints on her arm.

As I glance upwards I notice a tall man by the road. I shade my eyes against the sun to get a clearer image. As the sunspots flit across my eyes I recognise him. Quickly I turn to reinspect the fading red marks on my daughter's arm, hoping he does not recognise me. He strolled over with his still sexy swagger. I can feel his eyes watching. I can see them in my mind – cornflower blue with tiny lines at the corners that wrinkled deliciously when he laughed.

We were lovers then, a decade or so ago.

The heat starts at my chest and I feel it creeping its way up and flushing my cheeks. I brush some hair away from my face and wish I had made an effort to fix it before I left. He used to love my hair – running his fingers through it as we made love.

'Hello.' His voice startles me. 'I thought it was you! What a surprise!' I feel he can read my thoughts. I find it hard to grasp words that will impress.

'Hello! Fancy seeing you here!' stumbles pathetically from my mouth. I'm sure he can see how flustered I am. Looking down to hide my flushed cheeks from his gaze, my attention is taken by the children. Robert has raced back to the swing, seeing an escape from punishment. Daniel has noticed them. I wonder what he is thinking. Slowly he smiles down at them, looking casually at their faces. They looked like street urchins. Their straggly hair was not brushed and their noses were in need of a wipe. 'They look like you,' he remarked. Does he mean I look a wreck? I can hear my heart pounding in my ears.

'They are wonderful children,' I replied, feeling I needed to defend them.

I introduced them and, to my relief, Claire was very polite. 'Pleased to meet you,' she said, sniffing.

I scooped James up from his imaginary building site under the bench and put him on my lap, wiping his nose with the hem of his tatty T-shirt as I did, trying desperately to look like the perfect mother. Not only have I let myself go, but my children look neglected as well.

I know he feels it was a blessing we parted. I can see the disapproval in his eyes. He was never meant to be a father. It would not suit his lifestyle. How I envy him his freedom.

But I have made my choices.

Our dreams led us along different paths. I yearned to be a mother, to watch my children blossom. I dreamed of happy times, like those you read about in books or see in the movies.

We chat for a while, catching up with each other's lives. I can't tell him he was right, I spent too much time arguing with him in those days long ago.

He's sure I am happy – I have everything I ever wanted.

There are no promises to keep in touch as we say goodbye, just the light and airy niceties of acquaintances. With a sense of finality he walks out of my life again.

Listlessly I stare down at my feet. Dust has gathered around my toenails and dulled the vibrant colour that was there earlier.

Secrets

The bus pulled up with a screech. Roger swung on the stainless steel pole as he glided over the steps and hopped off the bus. It was always busy at this time of night. Workers from the city were in a mad dash to get home before the News. Roger was often tempted by the scents that filled the air from the trendy cafes that lined the street, yet there was no need to divert – Julia was a great little cook.

It was a balmy spring evening and jasmine scented the air with its sweet fragrance. The soft orange glow of the kitchen light was visible from the gate. An old bungalow had once stood here, but the developers had seen too much of an opportunity and snapped it up as soon as it came on the market. It is now a very tasteful Tuscan style duplex, with limed walls of a soft ochre and large windows overlooking the carefully shaped hedges in the courtyard. A terracotta fountain trickled quietly in the centre.

Julia heard the key turn in the lock. She was still in her white nurse's uniform but had thrown an apron over it as she had begun to prepare dinner. 'Did you remember the cream?' she called from the kitchen.

'How was your day, dear?' Roger mumbled under his breath as he hung his jacket in the hall and trudged out to join her. He pecked her on the cheek as he put the cream on the black granite bench.

'I'm running a bit behind,' she puffed, 'I had to stay back at work, someone called in sick.'

'Can I do anything?' asked Roger, uncorking the bottle of chilled chardonnay that had been waiting in the fridge and pouring it into two elegantly stemmed Krosno glasses.

'Could you chop the onion for me, please?' she asked as she busied herself setting the table.

'Do you remember David who worked in accounts?' asked Roger, peeling the papery brown skin from the onion.

'Yes,' she replied, as she gratefully took a gulp of wine.

'Well, apparently his wife tried to top herself last week!'

'What? Why?' asked Julia, her eyes wide with surprise.

'Well, you know how he left the company last year and everyone thought it was odd because he was going so well?'

'Yeah.'

'Well, Beryl reckons he was having an affair with someone at the office and had to leave.'

'Beryl's always full of gossip,' replied Julia sharply.

'Yeah, but she kept in touch with his wife, and she said he's been screwing around for ages.' Roger tossed the onion into the pan and gave it a shake. He added a bit more olive oil to the onions and they began to sizzle.

'Anyway,' he continued, 'he left her for a woman he met at a conference. They'd only known each other a month or so. The wife took it badly and swallowed a bottle of Valium. One of the kids found her on the bathroom floor!'

'Shit, those onions are strong,' said Julia, wiping her eyes. She threw in the prosciutto. 'What about the other woman?'

'Well, according to Beryl she's about 15, but she is prone to exaggerate!' Roger chuckled. 'He moved into her place –

she has a flat near the beach somewhere. The kids are staying with an aunt or someone. Probably the best thing – they couldn't move in with him, could they!' Another chuckle.

'Well, is it any wonder he left?' continued Roger, relentlessly. 'The wife was no oil painting. She probably did it because she was worried she wouldn't snag another man!'

'That's a bit unfair,' said Julia, steadying the knife as she sliced the mushrooms. She hurled them in the pan and gave it a quick shake.

'All I'm saying is, with a wife and three kids, it's no wonder he was screwing around,' said Roger as he put the water on to boil. 'I think we made the right decision not to have kids; they mess up your marriage. You wouldn't catch me screwing around!' he added.

'That's comforting to know dear. Where are the tinned tomatoes?' Julia asked, with her head stuck in the pantry.

Roger reached over her head and plucked them from the shelf. 'Domestic blindness, my love! I thought I was the only one accused of that!' he sniggered.

Julia turned away, choosing to ignore the ribbing. 'Can you put the pasta on when the water boils? I'm just nipping upstairs to change.'

Julia quickly climbed the polished wooden stairs. She drew the heavy chintz drapes in the bedroom and padded quietly over to the bathroom.

Tears welled in her eyes as she slumped onto the cool terracotta tiles. Opening her drawer, she lifted the makeup purse from behind the jumble of face creams and, pulling the red tassel, unzipped it. She drew out the carefully folded papers and, with trembling fingers, unfolded one. She smoothed it out carefully on the tiles and, glancing over the familiar handwriting, her eyes fell to the bottom of the page.

'We'll be together soon. Love David.'

Milk

Red hair pointing to
The nape of her slender neck
Arching swanlike
Down

Curving shoulder
Milky white,
Yet sprinkled with kisses
From the sun.

White satin
Slipping gently away
Revelling in
Abandon

The soft sheen of skin
Firm and supple,
Revealed in love
Shimmers

Over tender breasts and
In between,
A hand tucked in
Its softness sweet

Like the flow of milk

Sustaining.

ဆ

Stalking its victim
The panther's stance is crouching –
The sleek black Porsche leaps.

ဆ

Warm haven of love
For the two of us to share.
The bed – a warm nest.

ର

Warm and mellow sheen
Worn like a glowing gold band –
Rare friendship of old.

ဆ

Guardian with the black cape,
Dark keeper of the window;
Annoying blowfly.

ର

Clambering, clenching.
Vines entwined, struggle to hold
Lovers hand leaving.

ဆ

Purple haze at dawn,
Hang misty dainty earrings –
Wisteria blooms.

ର

Tender rosebud, warm
And cloying, gently lifted –
Bite the hand that feeds.

ର

Burning

The flame flickers to show
Its enduring gift.
Suspended oil warmed
By its ceaseless glow.

Misty scent rises,
Lingers – pervades.
It's floral beauty
Enwraps my senses.

Memories of purple fields,
Silver-green foliage.
Dry soil, crumbling
In strong, cracked hands.

Soft glow at dinner,
Illuminating every morsel.
Sending glimmers of light
Through glasses of wine.

Mother's drawers,
With silk and linen,
Squares of cotton,
Starched and fragrant.

Churches at dawn -
Candlelight glowing
Through open doors,
Inviting me in.

Memories wilt
In darkness.
Fading away
In a swirl of smoke.

Linda O'Doherty

Jungle Song

I gaze idly at a darkening vista. Waiting. Early evening stars have been flung haphazardly above us and a full moon has just begun to rise. It casts a pale yellow cloak in the warmth of the jungle sky. Kerosene lanterns are spaced regularly along the path. We follow them now as they guide our passage down a rickety walkway to the pontoon. There our canoe waits, bobbing in the murky Amazon waters. The dugout will hold seventeen if we sit close.

Our anticipation is tangible. It wafts around between us, animates our little group and makes us fidget and giggle. Our little group ... a motley assortment of characters with not much more in common than the keen sense of adventure that lured us all here.

Christine and I step into the boat first and Victor stands on the pontoon, ready to hand us in. Christine's from Darwin. Tall and lanky with cropped dark hair and a crazy raucous laugh like a galah. Infectious. I stumble in the shadows cast by the lanterns and she grabs my sleeve and cackles.

'Hey, watch it Charlie. You're a bit over-dressed for a swim, eh?'

The canoe rocks precariously as we step aboard and Victor steadies us. His grip is strong and firm. Victor is our tour-guide; short and stocky with a broad, smooth olive-skinned face – serious, until he's tickled by our foreigner's antics. Then he smiles, his big white teeth freed suddenly in an open-mouthed grin. His eyes flash and laugh at us, mischievous and wry. We've made it an unspoken challenge between us to elicit that smile as often as possible. I think he knows. He teases us – holds out deliberately until he can't resist it anymore and his grin bursts forth, delighting us.

Now that we're all loaded in the dugout our oarsman sets off. His paddle dips rhythmically, silently into the muddy water. He heads upstream. We are quiet for a while. Absorbed in our own thoughts. Melissa breaks the silence then, offering her bottle of red to Oran, who sits opposite. The celebratory wine is passed around the boat. We sip or swig according to our preference and the bottle is soon drained. She doesn't seem to mind. Melissa seems pretty easy-going. An army girl from Oz. Wasn't sure if she should've brought her gun along, she'd told us. I'd laughed. I imagined her shooting at tarantulas and snakes, and anything that moved a bit too quickly for that matter. Scary thought. I'm glad she left the gun at home.

Tristan has brought along a bottle of the local brew, which he also passes around. *Seven Roots* – a medicinal beverage, mildly alcoholic, supposedly aphrodisiac and faintly licorice, reminiscent of the vile-tasting cough mixture my mother once plied me with in childhood. Our sampling is cautionary and the bottle is returned to Tristan without its level changing much. Several members of our party have already experienced the unpleasant gastrointestinal consequences of over-indulgence.

'Hey Tristan, tryin' t' pawn the stuff off mate?' Melissa gibes at him from the other end of the boat.

'Yep!' He screws up his face, then places the bottle at his feet without taking a swig himself. Tristan's another Australian. A man of few words. He entertains us some evenings, strumming on his guitar and singing.

Erin asks if anyone minds if she has a swim. I fumble for her meaning until I realise she intends to swim naked. No-one complains. The oarsman halts the boat. Erin strips off her light cotton dress in one fluid movement and dives over the edge of the canoe, rocking us lightly. She floats around for a while, her pale beaming face lit up by the moon – an elfin, watery goddess. I silently salute her ethereal beauty. I'm also impressed by her blithe disregard for the piranhas she swims with.

'No problem,' Victor tells us. 'Forget about Hollywood movies with piranhas. They don't bother you. But better not swim if you have a cut or something. And crocodiles. Well, we have a species here, they are called Caiman. Do you know them?'

'No. What about the Caiman, Victor. Don't they bite?'

'You don't have to worry about the Caiman,' Victor smiles, flashing his big white teeth. He is baiting me, I know. He doesn't elaborate, so I take the hook

'Why not, Victor?' I grin back at him, enjoying myself immensely.

'Because we've eaten them all. Well, most of them. They taste really good. Piranha, too!' His smile is devilish.

Erin is ready to climb aboard from the stern. The oarsman moves forward in the boat so that Sidney and Richard can hoist her in. She does her best not to drip on anyone as she finds her seat. Erin stands slightly as she tries to wriggle her wet body into her dress. Melissa helps her, giving a few deft tugs.

The oarsman resumes our journey. Victor sits at the helm gazing out to the far bank, always alert to point out to us some new feature of his domain. His warm casual tone at these times betrays his feelings. He loves the Amazon and revels in sharing it with us. Victor is the grandson of the *Bora* people's Shaman-Chief. We spent a night at their village last week. They sang and danced to the primal pounding of drums. Then they pulled us all up to dance with them, hand in hand in long trailing lines. The Chief's first-wife danced on my right. When we'd finished she released my hand then turned and hugged me. Her weathered old face was brown and roundly segmented like a walnut. She grinned, warm and toothless.

'They don't live in the traditional way anymore,' Victor told us.

No. Now they sell necklaces and other trinkets to tourists like us. I wonder how Victor makes sense of life, standing with each foot in a different world. Does he judge us? Does he judge his people? Does he just take it all for granted?

The full moon has risen now, hovering brightly amongst a scattering of blinking stars. I wonder about the mystique such scenes of nature inspire in people's imaginations.

'Tell us a story, Victor. Is there a legend about the moon?'
I look up at him expectantly as he stands at the helm of our
canoe.

He glances in my direction briefly then shifts his gaze to
the moon. He murmurs several times in the back of his throat
as if questioning and answering, formulating a response.
Finally he reaches some conclusion and turns back to me.

'A story about the moon … Yeah. No problem. Do you
see those dark patches? I will tell you about it.' Victor rubs his
chin in a comic pose of thoughtfulness. He gazes upwards
again then raises his right hand dramatically in a cupping
gesture, as if he could hold the bright disk in his palm.

'The village people believe … ' Victor lowers his arm and
pauses while he looks around our little group. He satisfies
himself that everyone is attentive and then continues, 'when a
girl turns fifteen, it is a very special time for her. The village
has a big celebration. They prepare for many weeks, gathering
food for the fiesta and many, many cocoa leaves. When the
people chew these leaves, it gives them energy and power.
They hold a certain type of stone in their mouths, and this
creates a chemical reaction. It releases enzymes from the
leaves and produces this special effect. A man can travel many,
many days with no food or drink and he won't get tired. This
is very useful. The villagers will chew cocoa leaves and will
celebrate for several days and nights, dancing and singing
without tiring. This is a very special time. An important fiesta.'

Victor weaves his spell and we are hooked. He is a natural
storyteller.

He clears his throat and continues. 'The young girl – the
Chief's daughter, told her mother and father about her problem. In the night a man would always visit her … in her bed.'
Victor peers intently at us enquiringly. We nod, assuring him
that we understand his meaning.

Satisfied, he continues. 'After hearing her problem, the
girl's father advised her: "Next evening before he visits you,
take the juice of this special fruit (the *junipus-americana*) and
squeeze it into your hands. When he comes to you again,
touch his face. The juice of this fruit will stain his face black,

and then we will know who it is that visits you." And the young girl did as her father advised.'

Victor's knowledge of the flora and fauna of the area is impressive and he appears to know all the botanical names. He's wearing a UCLA tee shirt and I wonder if it is this university that he attended. It's not the time to ask him.

Victor pauses as Tristan asks, 'How long will the stains last?'

'It will last for about two weeks. The young girl did as her father advised and afterwards the man did not come to her again. But also, her brother did not show up anywhere. Nor the next day or the next. The brother was very ashamed to show his face, and was ashamed of what he had done. He decided to leave the village. He walked away – far, far away. He walked for days and days and he kept walking. The people believe that he just kept walking and that he turned into the moon. And this is his face. You can see the marks of shame on his face.' Victor raises his arm again, waving at the moon shining down upon us, its face all blotched with pale shadows.

Our oarsman guides the boat left into a narrow *sacarita*, a temporary tributary created seasonally by the floods. These are short cuts through the jungle Victor tells us. In the dry season the locals must use the main river. It's a surreal feeling, floating through the jungle. There are tangled masses of trees and vines on either side of us and we can hardly see the sky through the overhanging foliage. The flora seems oblivious to the fact that it's waist-deep in water. Whatever hasn't drowned is evidently thriving. Delicate ferns and razor-sharp grasses brush the sides of our canoe as we glide along. My lungs draw in the steamy-rich air. Thick, fragrant and green; I can taste its sweet mustiness. I inhale deeply, like a smoker drawing on a cigarette. I'm addicted.

Our oarsman halts the boat with a few deft back-paddles and Victor urges us to silence. He stands and raises a finger to his lips.

'Be quiet now and listen. You can hear nature's symphony.' Victor bows his head in an unconsciously reverent gesture. We struggle to still our chatter and become aware of the sounds around us. An orchestra is indeed playing to our little audience. The deep, steady 'plonk, plonk' of frogs creates the base beat, cicadas thrum a staccato rhythm and the high, tinkling bell of another species of frog pings steadily in sets of three. The vibrating hum of some unidentified insect fades in and out and even the annoying whine of mosquitoes adds a piquant flavour to this smorgasbord of sound. Somewhere in the distance we can hear the faint throbbing of drums. I listen enraptured, lost in the soporific song of the jungle.

Buzz Off

She laughed softly as she ran through tall dry stalks, her lithe body pacing easily – airy and insubstantial. A cliché in motion; ridiculously happy, like a heroine in the trashy romance stories she secretly loved to read. The warm, late afternoon sun lit upon eucalyptus leaves, making them glitter as if a sudden shower had saturated their dull, parched surfaces. A light breeze rustled through them dryly, giving lie to the illusion.

He was gaining ground, hot on her heels. She chanced a backward look and he grinned, mock-menacing, reaching out his strong brown arms stiffly in a parody of Frankenstein's Monster. She screamed shrilly, delightedly and increased the pace, her heart pounding wildly, her breathing rapid, audible. A kookaburra chortled obscenely somewhere in the tall gums that stood sentry to the clearing. He caught her finally about the waist, tumbling them both down hard on the chalky, sun-baked earth.

'Ouch!' she giggled and gasped, beating at him ineffectually, pushing at his chest with half-clenched hands.

His blue-grey eyes turned misty as he bent his head to her waiting lips. She closed her eyes. The drowsy hum of bees and the rustle of dry grass competed with a wave of seashell echo in her ears. She arched her body upwards, away from the punishing ground, towards the more satisfying hardness of his form.

* * *

It was later that the couple's awareness drifted back to their surroundings. The sun's warm glow was fading. The cool tendrils of the evening announced its coming, tentatively probing the spaces between their close-pressed bodies. She sat up, languidly.

'Hmmm ... chilly!' He grinned lopsidedly, crooked his finger at her and patted the earth beside him.

'No, let's go!' she smiled back at him, rearranging her clothing, pulling her fingers through her tangled locks. He reached out his arm slowly towards her face. He caressed it briefly and moved to her hair, pulling out a fragment of gumleaf. She laughed, opened her mouth as if to say something, then shut it again and pointed.

A loose, dark cloud had formed on the far side of the wide clearing. It looked as if it could have been smoke, twirling from a campfire. It soon resolved itself into a heavy, vibrating mass of swarming insects, writhing towards them. He followed her gaze; saw what she was pointing at. His eyes glazed over and his jaw tightened. His eyebrows drew inwards and upwards. She looked back to her lover and saw his anxious expression.

'Don't you like bees? I'm not that keen on them myself, actually. I remember when one landed on my arm as a kid, I just screamed and screamed. I held my arm out, stiff as a board, with my head turned away, just screaming. Stupid, really. I've never been stung, though. Have you?'

He peered at her intently, then turned away. 'I'm allergic,' he said, simply.

'Oh. What, like really allergic?'

'Yes.' He kept his face turned away, avoiding her eyes.

'Oh, dear. Well, shall we run, or ... what do you think?' She stood abruptly, glancing quickly from her lover to the approaching swarm.

'No. They'll just pass on overhead if we don't panic. Let's just sit, shall we?' He patted the ground beside him.

She slid back down beside him, her fingers fluttering over her clothes, smoothing them. 'I don't know … they're flying awfully low. Maybe we should lie down?' The hum of the swarm was now audible, growing steadily louder, tangibly vibrating the air.

'Yes, OK. Why not?' He pulled her towards him, tenderly, and they shifted around, then settled once more on the hard earth. He smiled, thinly. The swarm now droned sonorously overhead.

Eventually it passed. The couple raised their heads slowly. She smiled at him, laughed a little breathlessly.

'Well, that was easy. No problem. They're gone! Whew!'

He was trembling slightly; a little pale.

'Yeah, no problem.' He reached for her hand, squeezed it briefly, tightly. It was then that she noticed one lone insect settled on his shoulder, between his neck and the edge of his thin, white tee shirt. Her eyes widened. Her mouth gaped open.

'Don't move! Oh no, don't move! There's one on your shoulder. Oh, God!'

His lips tightened and sweat beaded on his forehead, despite the slight, cooling breath of the early evening that tousled his hair.

'Brush it off!' he demanded urgently.

She reached out her trembling hand, withdrew it again. 'I can't. What if it stings you? I can't!' Her eyes filled with tears; they spilled over, running down her flushed cheeks.

He grimaced slightly. 'Do it.'

She reached out again and brushed the bee's scratchy body. It rustled like a dry leaf then flew off silently. She collapsed onto his chest, sobbing.

He wrapped his arms around her, stroking her hair gently. A faint smile played about his lips. He laughed shakily and held her away from him slightly. 'Hey, you're making me cold!' A damp patch had formed on his shirt where her face had been buried.

'Sorry,' she mumbled, snuffling noisily. She bent her chin and gazed up at him through thick, wet lashes. She grinned wryly. 'Well, shall we buzz off?'

Neville Michael

Charlie Went First

The grave they dug me had no flowers.
Only polished sharp rocks
Separate me from the wild dogs.
The contrite scarecrows gather.
They offer prayers for my soul,
But God is a hard man.
He has seen the worst of Charlie Gray.
Perhaps he will let me in,
For I have lived in hell.
The scarecrows knew my shame,
They grew strong on their indignation,
I grew weak on their approbation.
The shame grew in my heart
Stealing my strength and sapping my will
Until blissful peace, torments end.
They saw in me, themselves,
And their weakness terrified them.
Look at me scarecrows!
You know you will join me.
I found Ludwig,
He and I are waiting,
Just beyond the struggle.

Jam and Cream

Grandpa always had bread, jam and cream at the end of his lunch. He was careful to prepare it just as he liked it. The bread was white. In those days all bread was white. It was freshly baked and delivered to his door before breakfast. It was sliced thickly by Grandma and sat in the centre of the table. A lace cover with blue beads on the hem was placed over the bread and the softwood tray on which it sat.

Grandpa would always make a great show when reaching for the bread. He would try to inconvenience us as much as possible. He would select the fattest slice, shake the crumbs off and slowly recede to his seat. When he was fully seated we would check our tea for salt and our soup for any other foreign object he may have placed there surreptitiously. Grandma would despair, accusing him of being childish, yet rock with stifled laughter if we were caught out by one of his jokes.

After he had resumed his seat he placed the slice of bread on his bread and butter plate and placed the plate squarely in front of him. Then came the process of the selection of the jam. He would speculate out loud about which of grandma's jam was better. The fig, he might say, was a late pick and therefore sweeter. Or the apricots were stolen from the neighbours' tree so the jam had to be eaten to hide the evidence.

Grandma and we kids begged him to get on with it, all the while enjoying his dissertation. Finally a decision was made and the appropriate jar passed down the table to him. The jam was always spread thickly, covering the bread from crust to crust. When he was done he called for the cream.

This was not 'cream' as we know it today. This was the cream of cows on good green-feed, milked on frosty mornings. It was the cream of hand wound separators dinging in a cyclic rhythm as young hands tried to keep pace. It was the cream of old steel ice-cream containers that sat in kero fridges and waited for the bread and jam.

When he received the cream he would spoon out a 'dollop' and trowel it over his bread and jam. The whole preparation now concluded he went to work cutting his masterpiece. Firstly on the diagonal, cutting from corner to corner. Then further slicing each triangle into two smaller ones.

Now, holding a piece by the crust and using his knife to hold the floppy point, he flipped it into his mouth. He crossed his eyes at the pure rapturousness of the moment and extolled that moment to be as near to heaven as he would wish to go.

Then it was our turn. We knew that the whole process ended with us sharing Grandpa's bread and jam. So he would dole out the small slices making sure he got cream on our noses.

Katherine White

A Chance Meeting

So this was Friday night, Tim Hamilton thought as he sat down in the alfresco dining area of a popular Rundle Street cafe. Not too bad, but he was only really here because he had nothing else to do. Chris and Joanne had persuaded him to come, they claimed he needed to get out more. There had been too many quiet nights in, ever since the accident.

His violet eyes safely concealed by his wrap around sunglasses, Tim's world was in smell, touch, taste and sound. He could breath in the aroma of freshly brewed coffee, and smell the exhaust fumes from the cars that were driving down the street. He was able to taste his coffee, which had clearly been made with Adelaide tap water. He could hear the band that was playing inside. They were doing covers of all old songs from the eighties. He ran his hands along what he assumed was a menu, but he could not read it. He could not see. Not since the accident.

* * *

I want to go home, Deena Andrews thought as she sipped her coffee. She was only here because there was another hour before the next bus home. She'd left home at seven thirty that morning, giving her three-year-old daughter a hug and making her promise to be good for Grandma and Grandad. Then, she caught the bus into the city, standing for most of the way after surrendering her seat to an elderly lady. She had been late for work and the boss had humiliated her again, shouting at her in front of the other employees.

Her ears were still ringing from his words. 'You're bloody lucky I employed you in the first place Deena. How many people in my position do you think would take on a single mother who never even finished high school?'

Deena was never bitter about her past, even if things had been tough over the past four years, ever since she had found out she was going to have Tamara. It seemed strange now, to think that she had once been a sixteen-year-old teenager, who's biggest problems were what to wear and whether her English teacher would give her an A for her last essay. Those days were long gone. She had to 'take responsibility for her actions', as her parents put it.

Still, as bad as her job was, she was earning good money, enough to buy Tamara some toys and clothes for her birthday. Since finishing work at five, she had been up and down Rundle Mall, trying to find just the right things. Now, as she sat in the cafe, Deena was surrounded by colourful plastic bags, all of which contained things that she hoped would please her daughter.

'What do you want most of all for your birthday?' she had made the mistake of asking Tamara the previous night.

'A Dad,' Tamara had replied innocently. Inwardly, Deena had groaned.

Ever since starting kindergarten and discovering that most of the other kids had two parents, Tamara had been demanding to know where her Dad was. Why didn't she have one? She wanted one. Deena sighed. It was a long and difficult story and she knew that she would have to explain it all to her daughter one day, when she was old enough to understand.

* * *

Tim thought about the accident all the time. It consumed him, Joanne had once said. It had been so sudden, and unexpected. He had been seventeen years old at the time. He was on his way home, after leaving Deena safely on her doorstep. Then, a drunken driver had come out of nowhere and driven straight into the driver's side door of his Torana. Fragments of glass had been caught in his eyes and the doctors said that the tissue had been left scarred, permanently. He would never see again.

The worst part was Deena. She was beautiful, with turquoise eyes and hair that was a rich shade of auburn. Most women had to dye their hair to get it that colour. But not his Deena. Her hair was real.

They had been together right through high school. They had plans. She was going to be a model and he was going to be a photographer. They were going to travel the world together. Big Ben, the Eiffel Tower and The Great Wall of China. He was going to photograph them all and then sell the pictures to other tourists.

But then the accident happened, robbing him first of his sight, and then of Deena. She had broken up with him. She never told him why, but he had suspected it was because of the accident. But these days he knew better ...

* * *

Tamara's father went by the name of Tim. Tim Hamilton, Deena thought with a smile. They had been high school sweethearts. She had thought things would last forever, but when she had found out she was going to have Tamara, things changed. She had meant to tell Tim, but the accident had happened before she had a chance. She remembers the night well. First there had been the phone call. Then she had rushed to the hospital. She had visited him every day and had done everything in her power to make his week long stay more comfortable.

Then her parents had found out about the baby. They stepped in, telling her that Tim had enough problems at the moment. He did not need the additional burden of fatherhood.

'And what's he going to do for you anyway Deena?' her father had demanded. 'He's never going to be able to provide for you and the baby; he'll be on a disability pension for life. You'll be better off without him.'

Reluctantly, Deena had ended it. She never told him why. He had been devastated. *He probably thinks I'm a selfish cow*, Deena thought as she sipped at her cappuccino. *A stupid, selfish cow. Which I am. I never should have given in to my parents like that.*

He had found out about Tamara, eventually. It was hard to keep secrets, especially when they lived only a few suburbs away. Joanne had seen her one day at the shopping centre. She had been hugely pregnant at the time, eight months gone.

That evening, she received the first of many phone calls from Tim. 'Are you pregnant Deena? Is it mine? Why didn't you tell me?' Then, after Tamara was born, he continued to call. 'When are you going to let me visit her? You don't have a right to do this Deena. You know I can get a court order …'

It had broken her heart. There was nothing that she had wanted more than for her, Tim and Tamara to all be a family. But her parents had different ideas. And they had been the ones to support her financially until she found a job. She owed them. She had to do as she was told.

Suddenly, Deena's mobile rang. She smiled, just listening to the tune. It was the theme from *I Dream of Jeannie*. Tim had programmed it for her. She kept it because it reminded her of him. Five years she'd had this phone. It was so out of date – it looked like a brick compared to all the different mobiles you could get now.

'Hello,' she said, knowing that Tamara would be on the other end.

'Mummy.'

Deena smiled at the sound the childish voice. 'Hello Tamara, what's up?'

'When are you coming home?'

'Soon,' Deena promised, looking down at her watch. 'Mummy's going to get on a bus and she'll be home a bit after that.'

'When?' Tamara persisted.

'Soon enough,' Deena sighed. 'Is Grandma there?'

'Yes,' Tamara replied.

'Can Mummy please talk to her?'

'Okay.'

* * *

In the distance, Tim could hear a mobile phone ringing. It was playing the theme from *I Dream of Jeannie*, just the same as Deena's mobile had. What were the odds of there being two phones that played that tune, Tim wondered. He had spent an entire weekend trying to get the tune right and then program it into her phone.

'Chris,' Tim whispered urgently to his friend. 'Can you see Deena around here anywhere?'

'Deena?' Chris asked. 'What would she be doing here? She probably has to be in bed by ten, you know what her parents are like.'

'Yeah I know mate, they're Nazis, both of them. It's just … I could swear I heard her phone … nah, maybe it was someone … '

'Nah mate, your right,' Chris interrupted. 'Joanne's just spotted her, she's a couple of tables away.'

'Where?'

'She's two tables to the left, right by the door,' Joanne sighed. 'And Tim? Please don't do anything stupid.'

* * *

As Deena put her mobile back down on the table, she was surprised to find Tim standing before her.

'Tim,' she said, staring at him wide-eyed and open mouthed. 'What are you doing here?'

'So I got the right table then?' he asked as he felt for a chair and sat down. 'It's a bit hard to tell.'

Deena took a deep breath. 'What are you doing here?' she repeated.

'What did you expect me to do after we broke up?' Tim demanded. 'Stay in every night?'

'Well, no. It's just … it's such a shock. I never … I never expected you to be here tonight.'

'I didn't expect you to be here either,' Tim pointed out. 'I just heard your phone and … well, I just want to know one thing. How's Tamara?'

He says her name with such affection, Deena thought. *It's like he loves her already, even though they've never met. He'd like her too, I know he would. She's such a good kid.*

'She's good,' Deena said nervously. 'It's ... it's her birthday next Thursday.'

'I know. Where should I get Joanne to address the card? For some strange reason I don't seem to have your address.'

Deena looked down at her watch. 'It's late,' she said. 'I have to get going or else I'll miss my bus.'

'We'll get a taxi back together,' Tim promised. 'You'll be home before your parents have time to start stressing about their precious daughter being out late.'

'It's not that Tim,' Deena said quietly. 'It's just I promised Tamara that I'll be home ...'

'Taxi's quicker than a bus,' Tim reminded her.

' Okay,' Deena sighed. 'What do you want Tim?'

Tim was quiet for a moment. 'Tamara,' he said finally. 'I think I have the right to know my own daughter don't you?'

Deena took in a deep breath and shifted nervously in her chair. *Of course he has a right to know her,* she thought. *She's his daughter. It's just my parents ... but what right do they have to say whether Tim can see Tamara or not? They're not her mother, I am.*

'Well?' Tim continued.

'Well yes,' Deena said as she jumped out of her chair. 'Now I'm sorry Tim, but I'm about to miss my bus.'

* * *

Clearing the colourful paper up from the floor, Deena smiled. Tamara's birthday had been a big success. A row of cards sat on the mantelpiece. Ten, Deena counted. *Ten. I hope she realises just how many people there are out there that love her.*

'Deena.'

Deena jumped, then turned around. 'Tim,' she laughed. 'You scared me.'

'I'll bet I did,' he replied. 'Where's Tamara?'

'Oh, my dad took her around to the park. He wanted to show her how to ride her new bike.'

'She's growing up.'

'I know,' Deena sighed. 'Five years old today.'

'A lot's changed in the last year, hasn't it?'

Deena smiled. That was an understatement. Everything had changed thanks to meeting Tim that night in the cafe. She had hurried away and he had called her the next morning.

'You don't have to have anything to do with me Deena', he had told her. 'Not if you don't want to. But I have the right to know my daughter.'

Deena had agreed with him. He did have a right to see Tamara. Breaking it to her parents had been hard. 'Tim's called. He wants to see Tamara and I'm going to let him.'

They had been opposed to the idea. 'Tim was a long time ago Deena. You should be looking for someone new, someone that can provide for both you and your daughter.'

This time, Deena had stood up for herself. She had taken Tamara to see Tim. It had been time to start thinking for herself. She had found a flat of her own. It was close to the city and to a childcare centre. It was also close to Tim. Tamara had started seeing her father every weekend. He was good with her, Deena realised. Despite what her parents said.

It had not taken Deena long to realise how much she had missed Tim. Once they had cleared the air about Tamara, Deena realised how well they seemed to get along. Then there had been the accidental meetings. Some days Tim would just happen to be waiting outside the office where she worked. Other times they would just happen to be at the same place. And then, it just kind of happened. They got back together.

Her parents had been angry at first, but slowly they had come around. As Deena pointed out, she was an adult now, capable of making her own decisions. If she wanted to get back with Tim, that was her choice. If she and Tim wanted to get married, that was their choice. And furthermore, what did it matter if Tim could not provide for her and Tamara? Deena could do that herself, especially seeing as she had just found another job.

'Deena?' Tim continued. 'Dee-na, you're not listening.'

'Sorry,' Deena apologised. 'I was just thinking, you're right. A lot has changed in a year.'

'For the better?'

'For the better Tim,' Deena laughed. 'Definitely for the better.'

Rebecca Burge

Just another soppy love story

God damn it! Turn that fucking music off. I'm trying to sleep.

It's such a fucking hassle just to hear the fucking birds sing in the morning. I just want fucking serenity all right, not the bloody 'Carpenters'. It's seven a.m. Oh fuck, someone get a gun. No one can tolerate this fucking noise.

Turn the fucking music off.

I want to experience this fucking moment by myself; I don't need any fucking encouragement.

What's the story morning glory? I'll tell you what the fucking story is; my morning is ruined. I can't sleep, I can't hear anything but the God damn 'Carpenters' singing their mushy sentimental pieces of crap they call songs and it's a fucking Monday, another week is beginning, another week that I have no control over.

I am not saying this, merely thinking it. I don't talk. I haven't talked for ten years.

I chose this.

What is the point of talking? The majority of what comes out of people's mouths is mindless drivel anyway. I would like to spare the world from hearing more crap being spurted out of another mouth, my mouth. People are stupid for talking. I am clever for shutting up. Today is a bad day though, as you can probably tell. I fail to see how people can fill their minds and psyches with garbage. 'The Carpenters' are garbage. My mother has tried to get me to talk. She has taken me to many people, important people, mostly people in grey vests and fine-framed glasses. They haven't had any success getting me to talk. With pens poised they ask me questions and wait patiently for a response. They are still waiting for a response.

Frankly it's a waste of her time and money. I'm not going to talk. I haven't talked for ten years, so why would I decide to start again now?

As you might imagine when you don't talk you tend to think of many things. I feel as though my mind can be turned upside down, inside out and completely suffocated with thoughts.

This is not necessarily a bad thing. Thoughts form ideas, ideas create change and change is as good as a holiday, apparently.

It seems my parents did not think. Thinking is essential. Why should you honestly get married if you are going to end it in five years, indefinitely? It's a complete and utter waste. Hundreds of wedding invitations, the envelopes for the hundreds of wedding invitations, menus, thank you letters for the extravagant and ridiculous wedding presents ... even the marriage certificate is wasted.

Those trees could have been spared.

Although, to some people, ensuring that you have enough 'bums on seats' at a wedding is more important than breathing out carbon dioxide and breathing in oxygen. Some people's priorities are so far out of whack. My parent's priorities were out of whack.

If we are not productive, we are useless.

Why talk about the weather when we are doing such a bloody good job of destroying the Earth's atmosphere? Why bother using *impulse* body spray (to ensure you smell nice for your boyfriend) if the CFCs are going to reduce the oxygen levels? Trees die, meaning we can no longer access oxygen, and we die.

I like girls. I like looking at them, but that is all. There is not enough love in the world for me to give some of mine to a girl. The first five seconds of a relationship where your eyes meet across the room are the only satisfying moments of the relationship. Here you have not spoken to each other, insulted each other or hurt each other. Every relationship will turn out like my parents' relationship. The first few weeks are harmonious, no money problems, no great differences; they are pure joy. Next, one is lying about a business trip to Bali, an exclusive business trip to Bali, with only the boss and his secretary attending. Then they are using their child as a thing to barter with and earn brownie points. The child is emotionally toyed with and stretched between the two parents as if it were a rubber band. And finally divorce papers are filed through the lawyer with whom the wife has had an affair. In relationships we lie to our partners and ourselves. Sex is merely for procreation. There is no pleasure in it and, sooner rather than later, we become bored with our lovers. They do not satisfy us anymore and we turn to the next pretty face that walks along. There is no fidelity in this world.

We are so fickle.

If we do not love and respect ourselves, then how can we possibly love and respect others? And if we do love and respect ourselves, how can we gradually kill ourselves, bit by bit, by smoking pot; cigarettes; drinking; snorting coke; injecting smack; taking trips and uppers and downers; cutting ourselves ... even sniffing textas and glue sticks for fuck's sake? By doing things such as this we are placing a gun in our own hands and slowly, sometimes quickly, but definitely surely, pulling the trigger.

We are not poverty stricken, nor are we at war with another country or part of our own country. We can bear as many children as we desire, we do not have to choose one child and have the rest destroyed because of our country being over populated. We can wear what we want to, as much or as little as we want to. We do not get savagely beaten or murdered if we wear the wrong clothes, show some skin or talk to the opposite sex. We have all these privileges and fortunes in our hands and around us, so why the fuck do we litter?

These are just a handful of my thoughts. It is exhausting though, thinking. I have a lot of time to think, I don't really do much besides it. Sometimes I feel as though I am the only person in the entire universe that thinks. I only have to go shopping at the local supermarket to find out that I am correct in feeling this way. I wonder if the customer realises that every plastic bag used to pack her shopping is a step closer to killing water life. Does our bread have to be packaged separately into blue plastic death traps? Is it really that necessary to separate vegetables from boxes of biscuits? Which is worse: a slightly bruised eggplant or a strangled duck? The tragic thing is that most of the population will kick up a stink about damaged goods, but when faced with the news of another native bird trapped and killed, the world is filled with anger and sorrow, when in actual fact it is this majority of the population who are the culprits.

I, for one, am not a culprit.

Politicians needing votes in the next election will pull out all stops to front a recycling campaign. They will borrow the popularity of a rock star, pop star, sports star or movie star to advertise the campaign and programs resulting from the million dollar campaign; but the very minute the votes are counted and recorded 'Save the birds' and 'Recycling is the way to go' is only a passing memory.

Is there really a God?

Can there be a God?

If there is then how can there still be a war going on between the Israelites and the Palestinians? Is God punishing them? Is it the ultimate devotion to God? I mean, they are fighting over the existence of God and religion in general aren't they? Whatever happened to 'Love thy neighbour as you love thyself' biblical garbage? If there is a God how can women be raped, animals abused and abandoned and old ladies mugged. If my mother answers questions such as these then perhaps I will go to church with her. Although she shouldn't be allowed into church. She broke Moses' seventh commandment: 'Though shalt not commit adultery'. And my parents broke their marriage vows; I thought it was 'till death do us part'. Yes, I have broken the fifth commandment: 'Honour your mother and father', but why should I? I have no reason to; they gave up on me, ignored me and started to concentrate on something else – their lovers.

Sometimes my thoughts muddle and run into one another, I think that is happening right now.

The concept of a 'flesh and blood' human being will soon be unheard of. We are already being transformed into robots.

Our money is in a little plastic card. The card has all our information, everyone knows our details; there is no privacy. We are all merely numbers (or codes) in a systematic, impersonal society. Do we even have to leave our houses and step outside to smell the roses? Practically anything can be purchased over the telephone or the Internet. What is the use of human interaction and connection? I choose not to leave the house. I find peace in my room with my thoughts. My mother sometimes drags me along to the supermarket and the bank and I find we no longer talk to people. We do not interact with humans, only computers. We're told where to stick our little plastic card and when to key in our code (which is our identity) and eventually finish the transaction.

I might get out of bed this morning; then again I might not. It looks like it's going to be a sunny day today. The sun will kill more and more people. How can something so powerful and beautiful be associated with something so destructive? There is just too much to worry and think about in the world and if I don't worry about it, no one else will.

It's my responsibility.

If no one else cares we will all be walking around slowly killing ourselves each day, and killing others, the wildlife. I am the prophet, somewhat. But I can't be the prophet because I am obviously not religious, nor do I want to be religious or have any faith. I also cannot really be the prophet because I don't talk. I have chosen not to talk, it was my decision.

Sounds interrupt my peaceful solitary life and my thoughts. Sounds such as 'The Carpenters'. She plays them every morning at seven o'clock. The people in grey vests and fine-framed glasses told her I could possibly associate my thoughts with music. It does not work. The lyrics: 'Why do birds suddenly appear every time you are near?' are so shallow. Give me a fucking break mother, how can I possibly associate my thoughts with such sentimental bullshit? I don't associate with this music; I despise it. Each time I hear the songs I become irate and begin blurting out expletives like there is no tomorrow.

Perhaps there is not going to be a tomorrow.

Rachel Green

Our sky is falling

Together we wept, myself and the sky.
Wept as we knew that the cows would still die.
Wept for the red dust and its child, the corn,
that withered in fields before it was born.
We mourned for income that we'd never see
and the plight of each farming family.
Some who had young'uns, who only knew wheat,
would move to the city just so they could eat.
Banks would take acres of blood, sweat and tears,
heritage beloved for numerous years.
Feminine frailty is lost in the flame
of bushfires and washed out with lack of rain.
This season, our last hope, failed to relieve
drought that killed capacity to believe.
And firmament now, your life giving cries
Come only to mock, as livelihood dies.

Jo Norton

Through the looking glass

Locked inside the glass
eyes tell a plot of escape
she leaves the mirror

Melancholy drips from the rafters
and floats through the shell of necessity.
Movement requires no thought.
Thought navigates a body of its own,
a body which feels a chill,
naked with nobody to view
but herself. She likes it better that way
but still feels she's being watched.
Melodies float through the air like
passing bubbles. None stay to watch.
Their sour beat fills her emptiness
like a puzzle, but lends no satisfaction.
She props herself against the mirror,
cringing at the mad woman staring
back. The glass frames her like a sad portrait.
Would they see it if she was only two
dimensional? That gift of life and lust
preventing them from seeing her torment.

11:39 am

Her shoelace was untied,
as always,
she had food smudges on her shirt,
as always.
But today, standing with her
bed hair and buttons mismatched,
she was not to be
interrupted.
Her fuzzy eyebrows and unbrushed teeth
were out of place between folds of
unexpectedly soft skin.
Her face, for once, held
no smile.
Her eyes, for once, held
deep thought.
We waited impatiently,
embarrassed.
Why had she done this again?
She continued to
annoy the shop assistant;
she continued to
count out the
six dollars thirty in
five and ten cent pieces,
that will buy the first
cigarettes in
three days. Next time
she's going alone.

Steph

We ate Chinese the night
her bulge became a baby.
I thought you were a boy.
I avoided the hospital,
then you ploughed into
our home. What accident is this?
Squishy pink, gummy crying.
How do you hold it?
Tiny digits, fingers twitching,
how clean, untarnished.
How different from
what created you.
You look like pieces of us
stuck together. Soon I looked
forward to seeing how
you change each day.
I was once like you
with forever to come.

Your booties turn
to sandals, now you
call me big sister.
I paint your nails in colours
I would never wear
and put your hair in plaits.
You try to cheat when we
play cards. Sometimes I let you.
I lose you in my hugs,
you tell me not to smoke.
Twelve years ago we'd
be best friends.
But now, sisters.
Even though it feels
like a dream.

Kevin Ludlow

Photo of my nephew

You smile at me, at anything I do.
I love that, pity you'll grow up very soon.
You have rosy cheeks and a tiny chin.
And inside your mouth, your teeth just begin.
You experience love, happiness and fear.
You're probably thinking your Uncle's pretty weird.

As I hold you in my arms.
With your blue eyes, you stare.
I think to myself, you still have no hair.
So to me you're a mini uncle Fester,
Which I guess is kind of cruel
But when you are an adolescent, you'll be saying
Uncle, why haven't you got any hair?

Little Red Chev

'I'm not going,' she said as he walked in the door jiggling his keys. 'Not in a fit.'

'I'll wait,' he said, sitting and picking up the newspaper.

'Well you'll be waiting a while, I am just not ready.'

Mary sat down at the table. She looked at him, really annoyed. He wore a smug face and a white garment. Ed shook his head as he looked at the intellectual *Advertiser*.

'Lawyers and politicians. It's the twentieth century! And you call yourselves civilised.'

'What's it like?'

'Oh, it's one big party, you'll love it.'

'I'm frightened.'

Ed placed his hands onto hers. He leaned in, looking into her blue eyes. 'I know dear, but you have nothing to be frightened of. Hell, you were a lecturer.'

'It's not fair, I still want to be.'

Mary got up and went to the fridge. She opened the door and got out a beer. 'How long can I still touch things for?'

Ed looked at his watch. 'You've got an hour to say goodbye. On the up side, you have an eternity to drink. And the best thing is, there are no side effects.'

Mary opened the stubby of Pale Ale. 'Mmm, I reckon I could get used to this part of death.'

Monique walked into the kitchen. She went to the fridge for a beer. She grabbed two and slouched down in the chair.

'My God Monique, what have you done to your hair?'

'Mother, don't stress. It's only dye.'

'It's a bloody disaster. Purple, orange and green?'

'Look Mum don't complain, you gave me the money.'

'Money well spent,' Ed said, still reading the paper.

Mary slammed down her beer on the table. 'Shut up you! And I am still not going.'

Monique looked at Ed. She smiled at the man sitting at the other side of the table.

'So who's you're little friend Mum?'

Ed looked at Mary. 'Are you going to tell her?'

'Ahh, finally they're coming to take you away.' Monique put her beer down and laughed. She looked at her mother. Monique looked worried.

'Monique I had a little accident today.'

'What kind of an accident?'

Mary turned her head in the direction of the lounge room. Monique got up and walked into the lounge. She could see a lady in the corner, motionless. Sparks flew out of the power socket.

'Oh no!' Monique ran towards her mother, lying on the ground. She placed her hands up to her face. She checked for a pulse on the side of the neck. Ed walked in with her mother. Monique turned around; tears began to fall down her young face. She got up and embraced her mother. Monique then stepped back and sat on the couch confused.

'I can still touch you?'

'She can only do it for the first hour of death,' Ed informed her.

Mary sat next to Monique. She looked at Ed.

'We go when I'm ready.'

Monique stood up and walked into the kitchen. She then came back with the beers. She sculled her stubby and opened the next one.

'How could you do this to me mother? Who's going to look after me?'

'You'll be fine.' Ed smiled.

'You know she's a real pain in the arse when you get to know her, you guys are in trouble.'

'Mmm, I noticed,' Ed murmured.

Mary threw her beer at Ed. It went through his body and landed against the wall.

'Monique! That's not very nice, I'm dead.'

'Good going mum, I have to clean that up now.'

'I wish I could have been a better mother.'

'Well gee, you could start by, say, I don't know, not dying.'

Monique walked over to the telephone to dial triple zero.

'Yes hello, my mother has electrocuted herself.'

'You know Monique, your mother will always be looking down on you.'

Monique looked at Ed, frightened.

'22 Current Drive, please hurry.' Monique put the receiver down.

'No way am I having her always looking down on me, what if I'm like in bed, or doing something illegal?'

'Monique!'

'Relax mum. But what am I going to do? I'll be alone, I'll have to pay the bills, I'll have to … '

'Be responsible Monique, my life insurance will look after the bills.'

The sound of a '57 Chev engine roared in the background. A bright red convertible came floating through the walls and stopped in the middle of the lounge.

'Whoa, nice car, can you take me?'

'I'm not ready.'

'Sorry, we have to go, there's no more time.'

'No, wait.' Monique went to her mother and hugged her. She began to cry on her shoulder. Sirens began to filter through the room as the ambulance got closer to the apartment.

Mary got into the car and the engine began to roar. The Chev started to drive through the wall. Monique watched her mother leaving. She ran to the front door and let the medical aids in. They ran over to Mary and began to try and revive her.

'Please mum, don't.'

The wall began to swirl a black and white spiral as the rear of the car was about to enter the wall.

'Please mum, no!'

The engine stopped, and from over the top of the Chev's back seats, Mary jumped. She ran towards her body and went back inside. She sat up gasping for air, exhausted. Monique ran over and kissed her mother, before medical aids pushed her away and took Mary out on a stretcher.

Monique looked at the wall. The car was still there. Ed sat

on the boot of the Chev. He sculled the rest of the Pale Ale and threw it to Monique.

'See you in a couple of years.'

She smiled giving Ed the thumbs up. She walked out of the house, realising how short and precious life is.

Observatory

When life bores me, I begin to observe.
A constellation of sun glasses.
Endless streams of hair.
Plants, flowers and Bricks,
It's enough to give you the,
Slits, in her trousers.

Bees buzzing around the trees.
The sun dripping colour in the sky.
The ocean embraces the bodies.
The needle that says,
'Hi.' Shy, and hiding in the sand.
Its intentions are to be a prick.

Bridget Doyle

Full Circle

I was detached the day I found an attachment.
I often stare up at the night sky when I feel most alone
and think; everyone else who looks up at the sky
sees the same moon. And with this I form an invisible
connection with both those that I know and those I don't.
My eyes became tired. I felt the rain on my face.
The night was warm, despite the fact that the clouds were
crying.
I shut my eyes to heighten the sense of the drops on my skin.
I opened my eyes just in time to see the sky crack.
I walked home in the rain.
The moon was full and it followed me,
watching over me, making me feel safe.

I was restless the night I found peace.
When I dream I see circles that glow in the dark.
They spin and then spin back on themselves,
much like our lives, which spin in one direction
to get away from another, but inevitably go too far
and have to spin back the other way.
Those moments of peace and contentment
that present themselves throughout our lives
are the moments when we find the balance.
The place where we don't want to move
in any direction because we have
just enough of everything where we are.
He trapped me in his arms and squeezed tight
so I would not continue to disrupt his rest.
The moon peered in through the gap in the curtains.

I woke content the day I lost everything.
Like I feared the moment vanished, and was replaced by others.
These moments since have caused me to yearn,
long for it to return, wondering which way I have swung
to determine which way it is I have to go to get it back.
But it lies in the past now. Gone but not forgotten,
and if I concentrate on it too much I will turn into
one of those fools who does not see the need to forget.
If I dispose of it, burn the memory,
like I did all the photos, I will turn into
one of those fools who does not see the need to remember.
I will learn to embrace my clown face.
When I stared up at the sky the moon was gone,
and the clouds were still crying.

I was doubtful the day I found new meaning.
The stranger told me it was OK to talk to strangers.
He said it didn't matter what I believed in
'If *you* believe it is true, then for *you* it can never be false.'
I set them down in stone … These rules to live by, which *I* decree.
(I don't know about the stone, what if I change my mind?)
I believe in the strength that comes through pain.
I believe in the power that comes through awareness.
I believe in the healing powers of love.
I believe in the connection of every living creature
that makes it so, if someone is suffering, everyone is.
I believe you *can* talk to strangers.
I believe in the importance of the moon.
I looked at the sky and the moon had come back.
I tried to trick it by taking a different way home,
instead I got lost …
Eventually arriving, having found a new way.

Fools' Gold

Down by the river, where we all pan for gold,
a boy was born there amongst the scrub, or so I'm told.

I am sure he had a name, but it was one of those names no one could remember. His life was remarkable, yet remarkably common. His story has become something of a myth, a folk tale if you like, forming part of history. History is, of course, just recorded stories that have been altered, glorified and polished so they shine like gold, when in actual fact they are just as tarnished as those of the present. This is one such reason why our protagonist questioned everything and believed nothing he read. If this renders him ridiculous, so are you for believing me. Everyone who recites their account of his life, tells a different story. I believe them all. But this of course is my version.

Like everybody else he went out in search of that which cannot be found. He, however, never believed in this hopeless fate, truly assuming he could pan the waters and find gold, but bear in mind this is a story about a fool. Throughout his life he was constantly fighting a battle between who he was, who he wanted to be and who he could never be. These internal battles, much like the external ones, like the GREAT WAR, would cause mass destruction, and would leave a void inside of him that would need filling. At these times he would go out looking for someone else to restore and replenish what was lost in the devastation. He would go out looking for love.

In his first major encounter with the opposite sex he realised that people kept their hearts locked up in cages of rib. This made the beloved untouchable and caused our protagonist to become disheartened at the notion of breaking through. In his second major encounter, he found that the serenades that would lead to the discovery of the key that would unlock these cages, was the same as the one that unlocked their chastity belts. For a short while after this realisation he would take the key, deceptively bypass the heart and head straight for the armoured underwear. Later in life, ironically some time after his racing hormones had settled down, he took on three lovers, one who loved him, one whom he loved and one whom he hated. The first two are easy to understand, but why the third, she who you will later come to see, could easily be considered the most important?

At age five he saw his father topple into the river and drown. So focused on finding his worth of gold, his dad never took the time to develop some basic skills, like how to swim, or breathe underwater. He never saw the value of his own life without having a means to justify it and consequently never realised the fortune that lay within, that drowned in a river of sorrow and doubt.

At age seven, the replacement father that his mother had found had a craving for small boys, our protagonist ripe enough for the picking.

At age fourteen, it looked for certain like he would join his father at the bottom of the river.

At age sixteen, he still stood.

At age twenty-one he met a man who changed his life. You may have heard of him, as he forms the centre of another reasonably well-known myth. It is the one about the old man who, on that night when the river was in the sky and we were all panning for stars, entered a sweat lodge and came out a child; having learnt and then unlearnt everything. It was this man who taught our protagonist how to speak and, having found his voice, he could then be heard. He also taught him to let go of the past, consequently instilling in him his distrust of history. The man revealed to him how the past constantly changes as we do and, since it is not fixed, it is not a solid truth, it is merely a story once lived, forever alive … but forever becoming a lie. So he emptied his bag of lies, which he had carried around on his back for so long, into the river and watched them sail away. What use is it to be burdened by lies?

Occasionally he would look around at all the other people at the river's edge, clutching their pans as though their lives depended on it. When he examined their faces he could see how they were all wearing masks. Every so often he would catch a glimpse of his own reflection in the still water and realise that he too was wearing one. In trying to remove the mask, though, he became aware that underneath he had no face. I guess, just like them, he never really knew himself.

It was also there by the water where he met the three lovers I mentioned earlier, one who loved him, one whom he loved and one whom he hated. For him it was often the first of the three that was the hardest to take. She loved him unconditionally and, in his most desperate moments when he would try so hard to deter her, defiant as always, she would still love him. Whenever he would get lost and become forlorn, it was she who would come and find him to bring him home.

The second of the three was unquestionably beautiful. She had wings that were arms and hands that were handcuffs. Once he caught her he could never unchain his soul from her side. She taught him how to love, but it was a love that was laced with pain because, like all truly passionate love, it was unrequited. She never fell from grace in his eyes because she never got that close. He was like the ocean, truly connected to and in love with the moon, despite its distance. He *worshiped* her, her body and her soul, but she never *saved* him.

The third he hated, only because she stood as a reminder of all the things he hated about himself. I'm told that often, when we dislike someone, it is really ourselves that we dislike through them. She became a method of identification, a way for him to see all of the things inside of himself that needed healing. That is why in many respects she could be considered the most important in helping him on his journey.

These three women never had a problem with each other, that is until they met. Even then it was not really a problem that arose, at least not as far as they were concerned. The three women forged a bond of intimacy that could never be completely broken, a trilogy of souls, him forming the space between. This union they used to their strength enabling them to accomplish what *one* could not do alone. They had the strength of three and became invincible. They fought each other's battles and allied themselves against the rest of the world whenever they felt threatened or in danger. Through their connection he learnt the timeless truth that women have found strength in unity. It got to the point where, when he touched one of them, he couldn't distinguish which one he was actually touching. Their synthesis highlighted his separateness and eventually made him feel more alone.

At the end of his life he climbed a mountain, surveyed the view and shed a tear that ran down a valley and formed another river, which people since have journeyed to in the hope of finding their gold. They foolishly ignore the lesson his life and his myth has taught us.

Because, down by the river where we all pan for gold, he never found gold.

Occasionally he found a laugh that provided warmth in frost; a moment of clarity where everything made sense; a moment of strength that pushed him forward; a moment where he found himself only to get lost again; a woman who loved him, a woman whom he loved and a woman who taught him how to touch fire and not get burnt; a riddle that kept him searching for the truth and the discovery that he didn't really need gold after all. He was sustained by the substitutes, which ended up being worth more. He was sustained by the *Fools' Gold*.

Juliet Rooney

Three Strings

One stands alone on a tightrope,
With her face brightly painted,
The crowd ogles her from below.
She is frozen stiff,
She can't move forward
Into the brighter lights.
She can feel herself treading air,
Retreating, stepping back
Into god knows where.

A violin string being grated on
By a small grubby child,
Is scoured into the air.
It's starting to crumble
And grow mould like cheese,
It's testing my patience,
Like a fork balancing peas.

A live wire lies on a cold, cracking street,
Its current pulsating underneath its tough skin.
How often we all step over its pain,
Avoiding its snake-like twists and turns?
How long will it squirm before it goes lame?
How long will it be before we all do the same?

On the Forest Floor

The sun ignites the forest floor in silence.
My voice falls deafly on the tiny red spider on my arm.
How could you have ears?
The leaves don't rustle to ask questions
Of the things we are hiding in the shadows and under
     rocks.
They live without a conscience
And they get by just fine.

Until the trunks shed their bark noisily
And it peels off and falls
Like dandruff on my shoulder;
Until you shed your baby snake-skin ways
And I say, concealed under your wing
In duck-downing warmth:
'Nature is wiser than us,'
And you just nod along.
Only then will I close the window
On the magpie's song
And crunch its discarded shells into the grass
As I walk up to your gate.

Writhing in the warmth of a single ray of light,
I listen to the butterfly's wings
Beating together like a drum,
And I know she hears me breathing like a typhoon
As one breath causes her to over balance in mid-air
And fall like a warplane into the shadows
On to the forest floor.

On the Wall

You're a silent witness to everyday routines,
Standing there objectively
Reflecting reality.

I look to you in solace,
In company,
In disgust, in glee,
In acceptance of the truth you return.

In the moonlight or the morning rays
Your critical eye exposes me,
Unveiling my frailty to the beholder.

I scorn your integrity
But appreciate that you're always there.
I trust you over spoken compliments and cautions
Because I hear your unspoken opinion in an image;
In a momentary glance,
Or an elongated stare.

Upstairs and Downstairs

Floating upstairs
With empty glass and mussed up hair,
In laddered stockings and garter belt,
Silk slip swishing as she steps,
Dreamily humming along with a sad song
That echoes through the hallway.

Tripping upstairs,
Up, up, way up high,
High as a kite to the dressing room.
She knocks and waits …
Her name etched in cursive on the door,
Pushing through at last
Into her happy hide-away,
Where the lilies never fade and die
And their cards with sweet words
Are in permanent ink.

A G&T to quench thirsty work.
A hop-and-a-step to the vanity,
She perches herself on the pink fluffy stool,
'Just dizzy from the perfume,' she says to the mirror
And it's stinging her corrosive eyes too.

She lifts a pearl necklace from a tortoise-shell box,
Both are gifts from a man she once knew.
Hanging them around her lily white neck
She looks at them blankly
Sitting cold and lifeless between her breasts,
Their lustre withering;
Like the one lily in the vase that is standing so proud,
But is rotting at the stem.

Her slackened mouth hangs, her lipstick bleeds,
As two strings of muscle pull from either side,
Pull from somewhere deep underground.
They pull her down like the pearls,
Into an empty gorge, downstairs.

Sarah Adams

The Candle

The flame is nervous, erratic,
Can't stand still.
If it had fingers,
It would bite its nails.
Or maybe it has just had too much to drink
And sways aimlessly on its wick,
Waiting to pass out in its waxy bed.
Watch now as it tries to stand still.
It is an old man,
In defiance of time,
Betrayed by his crooked body.
Or simply yearning for freedom –
Straining at the leash
That keeps it alive.

Pieces of You

I had never intended to be the one to walk away.
That wasn't the role you cast me in,
and I could feel your surprise on my back.
I was the more surprised, I think,
because I didn't know my feet could do that.
I thought you had trained them better.
You tried to make a whole person
out of broken pieces,
but I don't think all those pieces were mine.
If you look closely,
you can see the seams
where I don't join up.
And I think my body is now rejecting
all those parts of yourself
that you tried to graft on to me.
But I used you too, you know.
I leaned on you more than I needed to,
so that when I finally walked away,
it was with a limp.
I really didn't think I would make it to the door,
and you probably didn't either.
I stopped in the doorway for a moment.
Just to show you
that you were wrong –
I could stand alone.

Homecoming

I am going home.

The thought sounded foreign in my mind, like when you see news footage of a car wreck and think *that will never happen to me*. I remembered leaving my father's house with my head held stubbornly high and my eyes cast forward. I was on my way, and I was never going to look back.

* * *

The streets looked the same. I don't know how I had expected them to change. They say that you never stand in the same river twice. I wondered if the same applied to the backwaters, where the currents ran deeper and left less ripples on the surface.

There were thing you didn't talk about in my neighbourhood. Secrets that grew wild and flourished in dark places like mushrooms, and everyone pretended not to see. Like Judith Lewis' schizophrenic sister who drowned herself and her baby daughter when her husband left them, which everyone referred to as 'an unfortunate accident'. Or my mother, whose pale face was frequently coloured with violet blooms that she painstakingly covered with foundation, and everyone pretended those muted bruises weren't there.

As a child, I used to stand in the doorway of my father's study and watch as he listened to his Chopin records, his eyes closed and his hands conducting lightly. Those hands that caressed the air to the music were the same that reached for the whisky bottle night after night. The same hands that beat out the inadequacy of the man onto the wife who never said a word. I remember sitting on the stairs as a child, my cheeks wet with tears, my eyes closed against the harsh sound of his drunken rage and the crashing that followed. I would sit shaking on those stairs, my fist clenched white-knuckled around my father's penknife, praying for the courage to stop him. I never heard my mother's voice as he tried to transfuse his liquid hurt into her. It wasn't until the house fell quiet, as his low sobbing began, that I heard her voice. I knew that soft refrain – it was the one that had soothed my nightmares away, that had murmured comfort while her cool hands bandaged my scraped knee. And it was the one that nightly cleansed an undeserving husband of his sins.

I could never forgive him in the unconditional way that she did. On those stairs I would feel the hurt and resentment leaving them for another night, the easy way they released it, like a bunch of dark balloons between them. And I would gather them to me, the pain and hate, a chaplet of Ophelia's rosemary *for remembrance*.

And I never forgot.

As an adult I would fall in love with men easily, always artists, men who were skilled with their hands. I was enchanted by the beauty the gentle conjurer could create. And I was always the one to leave, before the men could reveal their hidden flaw to me. I carried my distrust close to my heart.

* * *

And now I was going back. I wanted to apologise to the young girl who had cried silently on the stairs, penknife in small fist, and to the young woman who had screamed the truth at him, just that once, and vowed never to return. I felt like I was betraying them. It was their pain too, those obstinate girls. But it was me, now almost a middle-aged woman, who had been the one to receive the news. *Liver cancer*. A young Clare could have stared in the face of his imminent death without mercy. She hadn't tasted life's other disappointments yet, hadn't known another hurt other than his. But I had. The line between black and white had blurred over the years, and now I was trying to make sense of the grey areas.

* * *

I knew that he was dying when I saw the autumn leaves scattered across his front lawn. He would never have allowed that sort of disorder. I wondered if he could see out his window as the world slipped out of his control.

My feet carried me up the path, when my head would have preferred to wait in the car. I retraced the familiar steps. *Step on a crack and you'll break your mother's back*. Only if your father doesn't do it first.

She was standing at the door, my mother, and a wave of homesickness washed over me. She was thinner than I remembered, and her face seemed drawn. She looked like a husk of the radiant woman I had once seen in her wedding photographs.

I embraced her lightly, her bones felt brittle and fragile in my arms.

'How are you, Mum?' I asked, as I pressed my cheek against her papery skin.

'Oh, a little tired. Your father refuses to have a nurse come to the house, and he won't stay at the hospital.'

Indignation flared. 'That's not fair, Mum. You shouldn't have to do it all.'

'It won't be for much longer,' Mum remarked quietly. 'Now come in, Clare. I'll put the kettle on.'

I followed her obediently into the house, flinching as we passed the staircase. She seated me in the lounge room and went into the kitchen to make tea. I looked around warily. I felt like someone had transposed me back into the past, but as a stranger. It all looked the same as I remembered it, a tribute to my mother's housekeeping. I could hear her moving around the kitchen, and I felt the silent, palpable presence of my father upstairs.

I wondered why I had come. For resolution? How could anything be resolved in a house like that, where nothing ever changes and everyone quietly steps around the problems without looking at them. Or was it justice I had come for? Like the witnesses to an execution, who hope that this death will chase their nightmares away.

My mother brought the tea on a tray, as if I was company, and we drank in polite silence for a few minutes. For ten years she had chosen her husband over me – she had missed ten years of my life – and yet we had nothing to say to one another. Because though we both knew the tune, neither of us was sure of the words.

'Mum – '

'Let's not do this now, Clare,' she said softly, almost pleading. 'There is so much water under the bridge.'

'I just want to know one thing' – *oh God, which question to ask* – 'Why did you stay?'

Her cheeks flushed pink and her eyes filled with tears. 'I love your father.'

And it sounded so clichéd. Freeze-frame her tears, paste her words as a caption under her face, and put it on the front of an abused spouse brochure. But I believed her. Because of that soft voice that drifted up the stairs and breathed into my child's mind that love is fixing the hurt. The skinned knee of your children, or the broken man at your feet who you made vows with. That was what women did. They offered themselves up as sacrifices for love. I looked at my naked hands and realised it was no wonder I had never married.

'But why didn't you ever stand up to him?' I asked, hearing the tears in my voice.

My mother blinked. 'I did, Clare.' I looked curiously at her as tears rolled down her pale cheeks. 'Why do you think he never hit you?'

I stopped at the top of the stairs; I could hear my blood in my ears. I didn't want to go in. I had wrapped my hate around me all my life. I would be naked if I forgave him. I could feel my mother's hope follow me up the stairs, but I didn't take hold of it.

I knocked timidly on his door but didn't wait for an answer before I pushed it open. The room was sepia-toned as the afternoon light diffused through the curtains. He was asleep in the bed and, for the first time in my life, I felt bigger than my father.

His face was gaunt and jaundiced on the pillow; framed by his wispy, silver hair. The bed was neatly made and the sheets were pulled over his chest, with skeletal arms in pyjama sleeves resting by his sides.

The door creaked behind me and the body in the bed

stirred, his eyes opening painfully. His gaze fell on me and he stopped still, not speaking.

'Hi, Dad,' I said softly, for lack of a more dramatic opening line.

He didn't speak, just continued to watch me in steely-eyed silence, and I felt foolish. I saw the chair that had been pulled up to his bedside and felt his eyes follow my gaze. His eyes told me I was not welcome. I crossed the room with defiant steps and sank into the seat beside me. His eyes spoke his mute fury.

'It's been a long time, Dad. And I don't really know why I've come back, to be honest. I know that you're going to die. But I always thought this was something I had hoped for, something that I thought you deserved.'

He flinched, moved his dry, cracked lips, but still didn't speak.

'So I guess in some way, I came to see what it would look like. For you to really be dying. And it's not as satisfying as I thought it would be.' The last sentence came out choked with emotion and I cursed my lack of restraint. 'I used to imagine killing you myself, did you know that? When you would hit Mum.'

'Get out.' His voice was dry and hoarse, but had lost none of its authority.

But I didn't know how to stop. For the first time in my life I could speak my mind to my father and he couldn't make me stop. I was stronger than he was.

'Did it make you feel good to punish her, Dad? What kind of man does that to someone he is supposed to love? Because she loved you, you know – and you never deserved it.'

'You were a child. You never could have understood.' He said it accusingly, turned it around like he always did, to make me the one who was wrong.

'What was there to understand, Dad? You were an alcoholic and you hit your wife. I know what went on in this house.' My hand clenched in a fist around an invisible penknife. 'God, Dad, everyone knew what went on in this house. They were just too polite to talk about it.'

He stared at me stonily.

'She should have left you, you know.' I said quietly, as I rose from the seat to leave. 'She deserved better than you.'

My hand was on the door when he spoke, in a voice that was resigned to death, 'I know.'

I closed the door behind me without looking back.

* * *

I dropped an orchid on the fresh earth of his grave, because there were some things that he had made beautiful with his hands. I didn't cry at the funeral but I held my mother's hand as she did. I never forgave him in the way I had imagined forgiveness to be. There had been no heartfelt reunion, no epiphany. It was a quiet revelation as I stood at his gravesite that, somewhere along the line, my hatred had ebbed away. There had been no flinging of those dark balloons of my childhood, or the cloak of my adulthood. No dramatic moment on a timeline that I could pinpoint as the moment.

I doubted that I would ever really understand my father, but maybe that didn't matter. As I stood at his grave, I could feel my younger selves standing with me, looking at the fresh-cut earth.

In this ground lies a man, and he was my father.

And maybe that is enough.

Biographies

Sarah Adams

I am a second-year Flinders Arts student, who has absolutely no idea what I want to do with my life. There are about seventeen thousand things I would like to do, but I have no fixed plans for any of them. In the meantime, I plan to do the things I enjoy, such as writing. I can get obsessive about using the right word, and will spend ages with the dictionary and thesaurus. Oh well, I clearly get a kick out of the simple things. I wouldn't consider myself a writer – writing is just something that I do sometimes.

Natasha Alexander

I am a third year Arts student, majoring in both English and Screen Studies. I never knew I would enjoy writing so much, and now want to make a career out of it. I have always been creative, both in writing and art – my two main hobbies, along with sewing. I grew up in the country, which allowed my imagination to flourish. I hope to travel and meet interesting people from all around the world. I want to experience situations that I can base my stories on, and visit landscapes that will become the picturesque settings within my stories.

Laura Bombardieri

Sometimes I stop and think about the human race. The species with the power, we rule the earth. Then, I think about our traits and the way in which we handle certain situations and I find it all so bizarre and complex. I hate the way that we are all clones of an image that society enforces upon us. I think that people have forgotten why they are here and they just do what everyone else is doing. Television dramas, sex, celebrity status, wealth – it is all here to distract us from what is real. I am yet to discover how one can escape from these distractions without subjecting themselves to chemically enhanced highs. I do however believe in one remedy; 'Dance when no-one is watching.' Discover who you are without confining yourself to social standards.

Catherine Bown

I'm a third year BA student, who has a passion for writing, singing, acting, music, and anything that's even vaguely creative! Poetry is by no means my forté, but I'll never back down from a challenge. I've lived in the Adelaide Hills all my life, but I intend to travel the world. I hope to one day write for the theatre, and next year will probably pursue further study, but I'm open to suggestions. I'm so glad that God gave the world writers to speak into situations, and throw light on the beauty of what it is to be alive!

Alastair Brown

I am around 170 centimetres tall, I have brown hair, which I often style with hair wax, and I have a 1-inch scar on my right knee. Born in the town of Reading in the United Kingdom, I moved to Australia with my family at the tender age of eight and I currently live in Port Noarlunga. I have always enjoyed writing, although my first love is acting and I am currently studying at the Flinders University Drama Centre. I would love to one day publish a novel, possibly featuring a turtle, six dwarfs and a hilarious misunderstanding about a basket full of dried prunes.

Rebecca Burge

I enjoy writing dramatic monologues because you do not have to worry about 'he saids' or 'she saids' and it can be a stream of consciousness. You also do not have to concentrate too much on the rules of grammar. I enjoy writing but I do not think this is where my true talent lies. I am to major in Screen Studies, with a minor in English for my degree. I am a volunteer at the local community radio station and present a show fortnightly. I am obsessed with music. I travel at least three hours daily to attend Uni because I live in Lyndoch, which is in the Barossa Valley.

Gary Campbell

Name: Gary James Campbell. Born 1964 in South Australia. Never wants to leave. Survived the Cold War, flared jeans and the Bay City Rollers with few scars. Addicted to the arts: The Simpsons, South Park, the Goon Show and the Hamsterdance song. Driven to Diet Coke and rice dinners by fear of middle age spread. Has been known to write letters to Kim Beazley about Labor Party policy. During lucid intervals likes to write, sketch, sing, dance and hike. Ambition: to write and teach kids (guarantee of perpetual impecuniousness). Hopes you will enjoy the anthology.

Rebecca Coles

I discovered my love of writing in late primary school, when I was required to create my own book for a class project. My first story was called 'The Magical Electric Guitar' and was a real success with my classmates. I decided then to become a writer. For several years I have been studying creative writing and drama, strengthening my skills, with the intention of becoming a professional writer of poetry, short stories and scripts. I hope to be able to inspire the imagination of my readers.

Sophia Coopman

Words. About me. What can I say to you in 100 words that will really tell you about myself? I can tell you that my name is Sophia Coopman, that I am 19 years old and studying what I have always dreamed of studying – Psychology. I can tell you that I write every spare minute I have, and that if stranded on a desert island, my poetry books, a blank journal and a pen would be the luxuries I would miss the most. And I could give you many more details, but I will leave the rest to my stories and my poems, between whose lines the real me is expressed.

Andrew Craig

I am the artist, practitioner of fantasy. I am the writer, who tells you what to think. I am the wordsmith, who forges your belief. I am the literati. My fantasy: Your reality. I am the illuminator, the instigator, the castigator. I tell you what to know. I am the master of words, guiltless orchestrator of your murder. But you're left holding the knife.

Katherine Doube

I am doing a BA majoring in English. I am a drop of water in a river that's flowing towards the ocean.

Bridget Doyle

I am in the final year of my Arts Degree and Flinders University, majoring in Drama. After completing High School I did a Media Arts course at Hamilton Secondary College. I came to Flinders initially to further my studies in Film and Media Production but grew an increasing interest for writing, eventually leading me to change my focus. Throughout my childhood I always enjoyed writing stories and see it as something I will continue with in the future. My other interests include visual arts and music.

Tim Earl

I live in the southern suburbs of Adelaide. I am currently doing an Arts degree at Adelaide University, majoring in English Literature. My plans are to write novels. My other interests include guitar playing and still life photography.

Nicky Graban

Writing is my creative outlet and something I've always wanted to be better at. Most of my time is taken up with family life, as I'm the mother of three young boys, with a fourth on the way. I took the opportunity whilst on maternity leave to return to study creative writing at Flinders Uni. It's been ten years since I completed my last degree at Flinders, and it was good to return. I'm also a part time social worker, so life is very busy. I plan to continue studying creative writing subjects and hopefully have some pieces published.

Stuart Jones

I was born in McLaren Vale, South Australia, in 1980. I live in the town of Aldinga Beach, not too far from McLaren Vale, and have lived there all my life. I have two sisters, and three very cute nephews. Currently, I'm studying my second year of a Bachelor of Education (Junior Primary/Primary Teaching). I have loved to write since I was in Primary School, and I will continue to write as long as I have a brain to do it. My favourite genre to read and write is definitely Science Fiction (and yes, I'm an ardent Trekker) although I also enjoy writing about personal experience, especially comical situations.

Kevin Ludlow

After several years of binge drinking and writing essays, poorly, my brain exploded into tiny fragments. I was left with one brain cell, called Herbert. Herbert is responsible for all my unusual creative ideas. Herbert is a thousand times smaller than a pea and has plenty of room to think inside my head. Through my eyes, he explores life and writes about life. He likes to write deranged horror stories and anything warped and funny. Herbert has aspirations of being a horror and comedy writer. Not really, but I do, so I continue to take the credit for Herbert.

Jennifer Lusk

I am a Valentine's Day baby of 1981, possibly the only truly great thing to come out of that particular decade. I began my illustrious career at the age of three with my debut short story 'The Spase Kruft'. I went on to pen such classics as 'The Adventures of Betty Buckles; A Day in the Life of a Shoe' and 'The Eye of the Cyclone'. I am currently pursuing my second passion of making a fool of myself in public by studying at the Flinders University Drama Centre. My writing has taken the passenger seat while my love of drama drives, although I am currently writing what I hope will one day become two best-selling fantasy novels.

Lise Mackie

Someone said to me recently that to be an editor you have to be a plodder. I laughed. It was a word I often use to describe myself and I was glad that my disparaging claims had some merit. I have no dreams of becoming a writer but, at 40, to have the chance to edit a book was a task I am glad I kept plodding for. I am thankful to see it come to fruition.

Christa Mano

As a full-time mother of two gorgeous boys, wife, full-time student, part-time worker and part-time small business operator, there isn't much time left over to do the really interesting stuff in life like writing stories and poems. One of my favourite periods in life has been the three years I have spent at uni. The biggest surprise is that I can actually write stuff that some people thought was good and the encouragement of peers and lecturers has given me the courage to continue. My inspirations are music, scenery, weather and interesting people. Rather than write the great Australian novel, I would like to write stories (long and short) about the art of living life. Life is short, we only get one crack at it and it's up to us to enjoy it.

Annie Maynard

I was born in 1981 and am currently studying at the Drama Centre at Flinders University. I have a strong affiliation with the arts and am passionate about social justice issues. Most of my creative written work has been poetry and poetic prose. I hope to branch into writing for performance and enjoy a prolific career as both a creator and a performer.

Neville Michael

I was born in Snowtown SA and entered Uni as a mature age student in 2000 after 26 years a farmer. I enjoy writing and all aspects of the creative process. I was the third prizewinner in the Spartacus short story competition in 2001.

Jo Norton

To most people I am a twenty-one-year-old arts student drawing my studies to a close. But to the international organisations to whom I am indispensable, I have an entirely different identity. I have the strength and mind power to shatter a man's bones to dust and superhuman powers that enable me to telepathically read minds and travel vast distances in a split second. My therapist insists I have a 'Wonder Woman' complex, but I know the truth and will give my life to protect it. Yours in peace and trust. X.

Linda O'Doherty

I'm in my mid-thirties, married and have an eleven-year-old daughter. I'm studying for a Bachelor of Arts at Flinders and am in my second year. I will major in English and Anthropology, which I study at Adelaide University. I love to write and travel. I'd like to do something in the future that incorporates these two passions. Different cultures fascinate me – what makes us unique and what do we share? I'm interested in what makes us tick.

Juliet Rooney

Who is Juliet Rooney? Mmmm ... What to say to make me sound lovely and literary ... Well, I'm contradictory because I do know what to say. I'm sweet, amusing, lazy, fussy, thoughtful. Sometimes I'm stupid, cowardly, self-absorbed and sly. I'm superfly, superbad, supersonic. I'm naive, brainless, rude, intellectual, tactless, distant. I'm passionate and cold. Shallow, but temperamentally deep. Loyal, witty, observant. I'm a stuttering sophisticate. Vain and insecure. Dreamy and spontaneous. Bossy, annoying, creative. Gorgeous in the right light. I'm feminine and masculine. I run hot and cold. Love me or sod off. I'm a million things just like you, and for enjoyment and therapy, to make sense of this crazy world ... I write.

Edwina Stark

The first story I ever wrote was about an ice skater who won a medal at the Olympics. Since prep, I have broadened my writing subjects to include all those characters I have met in the past 22 years: everyone from the common uni student to the sleaze in the local bar. Having almost completed my law degree, I plan to travel in order to expand my knowledge and, consequently, my writing skills.

Hugh Sullivan

I am twenty years old and studying for a BA, majoring in Screen Studies. The origins of my two stories – both having no grounding in real life experience – may be traced to the common fear that things will not turn out as one would have liked. What I may at times experience as a fear of the future, then, is projected onto the protagonist as a fear of the present or recent past; of a life not yet lived.

Katherine White

I was born in 1981 and currently reside in Morphett Vale. My first published story, 'Where's Jack', appeared in the *Advertiser* in 2000, as a part of the annual summer short story competition, and I am determined that it will not be my last. Presently I am halfway through a BA and am contemplating a major in either English or Legal Studies. Other interests include spending time with friends, shopping for shoes, complaining about public transport and finding ways to avoid the gangs of angry geese that are often seen loitering around the Flinders University pond.

Simone Wise

Hi, I'm Simone, I'm nineteen years old and in my second year of a BA. My major is Screen Studies, with English as my minor. My ambition isn't to be a writer, but this subject has certainly made me admire those who do get their work published! The story I've submitted – 'The Sports Lesson', is about my biggest fear. I loathed sports lessons at school. The story is completely autobiographical – the only thing I changed slightly was the teacher's name!